Books by Amanda Hamm

Eve's Brother

More Love in Andauk #3

Amanda Hamm

ISBN: 978-1-943598-24-3

1

*P*lans for the dining room that wasn't a dining room would need to wait. Eve dropped her still-blank notebook on the carpet and pushed herself off the floor. She waved to her brothers, Matt and James, as she passed through the kitchen. They were setting up a board game but looked up long enough to say goodbye.

She grabbed her coat and purse from a hook near the back door before she slipped outside. The old house had a detached garage her parents used. There was extra driveway between the house and garage where Eve parked. She had shared the space with Simon, or rather his car, before he moved out. It was easier to back out now that she didn't have to stay perfectly on her side.

When Eve parked behind St. Jude's church, the radio DJs had just hinted that an unbelievable story was coming up after the next song. She was tempted to stay in the car to wait for it. She might have done that if a better song had started. Instead, she jumped out to meet Emily, who had just gotten out of a minivan next to her.

"Hi, Emily. Are you here by yourself?"

"Yeah. Joseph was feeling tired tonight. He said he'd rather stay home with the kids."

Eve considered her 2-year-old nephew. "Being home with three little ones is restful?"

Emily laughed. "No. But it… it takes a different kind of energy than serious discussion." She gestured towards the school where they were headed to meet the other young adults.

"You expect serious discussion tonight?" Eve asked. She opened the door for Emily, and they both waited for Ella and Sebastian to catch up. Sebastion was carrying baby Matthew in his car seat. The meetings almost always had some serious discussion. And they almost always included some joking and random tangents. It was difficult to predict which way the overall tone would lean.

"Maybe." Emily smiled at Eve's doubts. "Given that I spend most of my days pointing out and naming colors, reading simple books I have memorized, and pretending to eat the same fake foods over and over… sometimes anything that requires my brain to turn on feels like a serious discussion."

"Matthew slept through the night every day this week," Sebastian said, "so I think we can turn our brains on, too."

Ella nodded in agreement.

"That's wonderful," Emily said.

Eve smiled. She trailed the others down the hallway. She felt slightly out of place since she had no kids. But she knew there would be other single people once everyone had gathered.

Jessica and Isaac were setting up the hallway play area with their kids already inside it. Emily, Ella and Sebastian stopped to chat while Eve ducked into the room. Chairs were already set in a circle. Gabriel and Ruth usually led the meetings, and they appeared to be going over notes for the evening. Heather and

2

Adam were sitting next to them browsing their phones. Tori was sitting by herself on the other side of the room. Eve claimed the seat next to her, trying not to care that it left only one opening for someone to sit next to her.

"Hi. Apparently, you did *not* convince Simon to come tonight."

Tori shook her head. "Same conversation as always. 'Why don't you come?' 'Maybe next week.'"

Eve pulled out her phone. "I'll tell him to put next week on his calendar." She sent a text and then put it back in her bag. She looked at Tori and tipped her head towards their leaders. "Any hints on what – or I guess I should say who – is the topic for the night?"

They used a different saint each week to jump-start a discussion. Tori shrugged before the room got louder. Everyone from the hallway streamed in with a few extra bodies and voices. Ben Shannon was near the end of the crowd. He noticed Eve and moved towards the seat next to her. She quickly resumed her conversation with Tori to seem less aware of his movement.

"I'm watching Spencer for a bit on Saturday morning."

"Oh, he's so cute," Tori said. "Just him and not the little one?"

"Anna's taking the baby with her." Anna was Eve's sister-in-law. Her second baby was only about a month old. Eve and her mom had watched the first one several times recently to help with the adjustment. "I think I'll take Spencer to the library," Eve said. "I won't have a car seat, and it's about the only place close enough to walk. Do you think someone too young to read would still be entertained by that?"

3

Tori nodded. "I think anything new to look at will keep him happy for a while."

"That's my hope." Eve turned to Ben to say hi.

"What did Dan say?" he asked.

"Uh… about what?"

"You haven't seen the comments about how much extra people are willing to pay?"

"Not yet." Eve worked at Pans and Plates, a pizza place owned by her uncle Dan. He let her manage some social media for the restaurant. She kept the notifications off and tried to check in only on her schedule. Sometimes that was more frequent than others. At the moment, she was glad to be missing something. She was happier hearing it from Ben.

"It's hard to tell how serious anyone is," he said, "but bids have gone up to fifty bucks extra for a Christmas pizza like the picture."

"Wow. Now I'm curious what Dan will say, too." She smiled as she looked forward to seeing those comments herself. Her cousin Noah, who also worked at Pans and Plates and was Dan's son, was constantly trying to come up with something new. He'd been working on a Christmas pizza, speculation for which had given her great fodder for posts. Dan and Noah eventually agreed to a promotional Christmas pizza that would have a crust speckled with broccoli bits and topped with plenty of spinach and tomato to give it a red and green look.

Noah had artfully arranged one pizza so the toppings were shaped like a wreath of holly. Eve had posted that picture with the announcement and a very clear disclaimer that the actual pizza would have the toppings piled on like a "normal pizza" because Dan wasn't about to waste time on frivolous decoration.

4

"I said ten bucks," Ben said with a smile.

"And how serious were you?"

"Serious enough, considering I know Dan won't do it for ten."

Eve laughed at what she knew was intended to make her laugh, then sat back to better include Tori in the conversation. "Do you think he'd do it for fifty?"

"Probably not. It might encourage Noah."

They all laughed as Noah walked in. He glanced her way with his eyes slightly narrowed as though he suspected the reason for the amusement on her face. Sarah, Jackson and Cassidy arrived with him. Jackson and Cassidy had been dating a few months and Eve guessed that Sarah had recently agreed to date Noah. He refused to confirm it, but he was less cranky about not confirming it than he used to be, and Eve hoped that confirmed it. The chairs had filled so Jackson and Noah remained standing by the door.

"Cue the notebook in three… two… uh… one and a half…"

Eve smiled at Ben's attempt at a countdown. Gabriel had a habit of flipping open his notebook somewhat dramatically to signal the start of a meeting. Even if he'd just been looking at it with Ruth, he'd flip the lid closed to open it again. It usually got everyone's attention – in part because they knew to watch for it – and was less annoying than other methods he could have used.

"One and a quarter… I think Ruth distracted him."

Cassidy heard as she crossed in front of Ben for a seat. She snorted at the excuse for his failure.

"Should I try again? Let me get his attention." Ben waved at Gabriel.

Gabriel was looking a different direction and opened the notebook without a countdown. That was for the best. Eve had enough trouble keeping a straight face during the opening prayer.

"Okay, gentlemen, follow me," Gabriel said.

Ben stood to join the other guys in a classroom across the hall. He met Eve's eyes as he did. "I'll call you later to compare notes."

She nodded eagerly. Eve missed some of the meetings when she had to work on Fridays. Ben had been calling her to fill her in on the saint discussed without her. When she was there, they still enjoyed comparing how the topic was discussed differently by the men and the women. They usually found a few overlapping points as well.

As the last of the guys trailed out the door, Eve realized that Tori had heard Ben say he would call her.

"Sometimes the guys take the questions in a completely different direction," she said. "It's really interesting to see if we talked about any of the same things when we start with the same questions. You can mention that to Simon next time you talk to him about joining us."

Luckily for Eve, Ruth called everyone's attention before she started talking about how she knew she could talk to Noah about the meetings because that might have made Tori suspect a guilty conscience was behind the babbling. Eve had nothing to feel guilty about.

"We're going a little... um..." Ruth paused to reword. "We picked an Old Testament guy who isn't strictly a saint because Old Testament people aren't traditionally given the title even when... I mean Moses was at the transfiguration, and we still don't call him St. Moses."

6

"No one's going to tell on you, Ruth," Jessica teased.

"Oh, I know. I just wanted to clarify." Ruth read from notes on her phone. "Zerubbabel helped rebuild the temple in the book of Ezra. This was after the Babylonian exile, and rebuilding the temple was important to the Jewish people to restore the proper worship of God. For our first question, I'm going to ask everyone to name a place that has significance – religious or otherwise – to you. Or to people in general. Let's go around the room on this one." Ruth nodded to Ella, who was on her right, to start.

Ella's eyes darted around the room while she thought of an answer. "I... um... cemeteries. People can mourn or remember loved ones anywhere, but going where they're buried is... special."

Heads nodded and eyes moved to the next woman in the circle, who said home was important, not just as shelter but an anchor of sorts. That was followed by more nodding. Eve's brain churned for answers. The meetings were low-key, but when they went around the room like this, she felt pressure to have a unique answer ready. She wanted to think of at least two in case someone took hers.

Jessica said St. Jude's was significant to her for religious reasons and personal ones since she and Isaac were married there. Emily agreed and playfully accused her of stealing her answer. Cassidy mentioned her shop, Granny's Shelf, because of the constant reminders of her grandmother, from whom she had inherited it. And then it was Eve's turn.

"I want to say the lake is my place, but... uh... there's a kind of embarrassing story about why." Eve glanced around to see if anyone seemed impatient. "Do we have time for a story?"

"Oh, yeah." Emily agreed enthusiastically. "We love embarrassing stories, don't we?"

7

The room filled with encouraging nods and smiles.

"Okay, so I don't remember exactly how it happened, or I mean, what he said exactly. But somehow, when I was really little, my dad gave me the impression that God lived on the other side of the lake. I think, based on conversations with him since, that he was trying to impart some deep wisdom about how we knew the lake had a shore on the other side even though it was too far away to see because we could see that it kept the water from falling off the other side of the world and that's sort of like how we know God is there even when we can't see him because we can see some of his effects."

No one appeared confused so Eve guessed she'd explained it at least as well as her dad had.

"But," she continued, "I was too young to understand the metaphor and thought he was telling me that God lived on the other side of the lake. So every time we went to the beach that summer and I think the next one, too, I kept trying really hard to see God across the lake."

"Do you remember when you realized that wasn't possible?" Jessica asked.

Eve shook her head. "No. I think it must have somehow dawned on me gradually. I think I matured from one summer to the next or something, and I just remember looking across the lake the same way, but knowing that I wouldn't see him. I still liked to sort of feel the, uh, vastness of him when I could look farther than I could see. If that makes sense."

"I love that story," Cassidy said. "I'm going to the lake this Sunday to look farther than I can see. That sounds cool."

"But it's cold," Heather said.

"Yeah? Have you never been to the lake in the winter?" Emily asked.

Heather seemed a little confused by the idea.

Eve was also rather surprised by the thought. She'd only been to the lake in the summer even though she'd always lived only a few miles from it. She wondered how it might look different and missed how Ruth got everyone back to listing significant places.

Tori said that a place special to her was the house where she grew up. She moved when she was starting high school and felt a sense of loss when she passed the old house knowing that she couldn't go inside. The next lady said she felt the same way about a house her parents recently sold, not realizing how the house itself meant anything to her until she couldn't go back. Some brighter examples followed and brought the circle back to Ruth.

"Restoring the temple took many years," she said. "I tried to figure out exactly how many, but there was a break where work was halted for like unrest or something, and I wasn't sure if some of the calculations included the years without progress. Also, BC math sometimes hurts my brain when the numbers go backwards, so I don't want to give a specific number if it might be wrong. Anyway, years.

"But the point is that it was important enough to the Jewish people to get it done despite the time and… In the book of Haggai, chapter two – this is where I get to sound like I know what I'm talking about – God assures his people of his presence in the completed temple, which made everything worthwhile. He said, 'I will fill this house with my glory,' and also, 'in this place I will give you peace.' And now our next question – and we don't have to go around the room, anyone can answer – is what is something that is

9

worth investing significant time, maybe even years or decades on? Either something you have done or are still working on?"

"Learning a new skill is always worth the time it takes," Emily said. "I remember when Joseph first suggested I teach some classes at the gym. I wondered about his sanity. I made some friends help me practice and was a nervous wreck before my first class. But now that I've been doing it for a few years, I feel like I'm pretty good at it. And it's so fun."

"Yes. Practice is worth the time." Bethany nodded. "I play the piano, and I learned to play some recognizable tunes. And now I – I've never practiced enough to be great or anything – but the songs I know seem easy now, and it's so much more fun than when I was trying to remember all the notes."

"I agree with practice. And I'm going to add relationships to the list."

"Of course. Investing time in a relationship is very important."

"As probably the longest married…" Jessica glanced around the room as she calculated the truth of her statement. "I can say relationships do always need deliberate, or intentional maybe is a better word, time. Isaac and I have occasionally gone days or even weeks feeling like we haven't had a real conversation even though we live in the same house because he's at work or the kids need our attention or we're just too tired. It feels good when we talk and remind ourselves we need to do that."

"Investing time also helps you really know someone," Emily said. "I remember Joseph gave me a little present right before we got married that… it was just this little plastic cake with a screaming face and there's a whole story, but… the fact that he knew I'd like it was more important than the actual present. When you know

10

someone… I mean, you can't know someone like that without spending time together, and… well, it's worth it."

Eve nodded along with everyone else. She knew time was missing. She also knew the desire to spend that time was missing. And it wasn't just her.

"Time isn't only important in romantic relationships." Ella spoke quietly, and the room stilled as everyone tried to listen. "My brother and I mostly ignored each other when we were little because he's much younger. But as adults, we've spent some time together, and I discovered I *like* having a brother." Her eyes moved to Cassidy, who was dating Ella's brother. "But you don't have to tell Jackson I said that."

Cassidy was already smiling before everyone else laughed.

"She's going to tell him," Eve said.

"I might." Cassidy's eyes twinkled. "But I was actually thinking I bet the guys aren't talking about relationships right now."

Her comment got another chuckle. It was followed by a few facetious suggestions of what the guys might be discussing, like investing time to bulk up their muscles or fling darts at a target. Ruth had a few more questions and apparently at least one she didn't get to before the time was up.

Eve wished the meetings were longer. The two girls she spent the most time with in high school had gone away for college and quickly faded from her life. She loved this time spent talking to females other than her mom. But she knew the women in the group who had young children wouldn't want to stay any later. She walked out of the room trying to be grateful for the time they did have.

The door across the hall opened. Ben was not among the first few guys to leave. Eve didn't wait for him or anyone else. She

11

drove home mulling over some of the thoughts that had been shared.

Her little brothers – both of whom were now taller than she was – were still staring at a board full of tiny pieces. Her mom was on the phone. "Dad says hi," she said.

Eve smiled. "Me, too." She heard her mom relaying the greeting as she continued out of the room. Her dad's job required occasional travel, and seeing her mom on the phone with him when he was out of town was common. She went upstairs to get comfortable.

Eve set her phone on top of the dresser while she changed into pajamas. The screen stayed dark. She left it there while she went down the hall to brush her teeth, but she walked back to take a peek in the middle. She hadn't missed any calls while she was flossing. She washed her face and pulled the headband from her hair.

When she returned to her room, she sat on her bed next to her phone before she noticed her bible wasn't on the nightstand. She searched the house until she found it on the game shelf. She had read only a few paragraphs before she felt the vibration. She picked up her bookmark and set the bible aside slowly. He didn't need to know how eager she was.

"Hi, Ben." She might have sounded too happy so she took a little breath to stay calm.

"What was the most off-topic thing someone said tonight?" he asked.

That was a common question between them. Eve was ready with an answer. "Chocolate."

"Chocolate?" There was amusement in his voice.

"We were talking about the temple, and then all of a sudden we were talking about whether chocolate tastes better when it's solid or hollow. I *think* it had something to do with how chocolate can be molded into different shapes and the shape of the temple even though no one said anything about a chocolate temple. I'm not sure how it was connected."

"What's your vote on that?"

"I like it when it's hollow so it can be filled with caramel or something."

He didn't say anything, and Eve didn't know if he was conceding her point or deciding whether or not it was worth arguing.

"What were some of the guys' answers to the question about things that are better when you invest time into them?"

"Uh…" He sounded more confused than forgetful.

Eve tried to remember exactly how the question had been worded. Maybe she hadn't said it right.

Ben caught on first. "Oh! The temple took years and… right. We mostly talked about building a relationship with God, how the more you give *to* him, the more you seem to get *from* him. We talked about how he always pours all of himself towards us, and it's our responsibility to keep up our end in order to receive that grace and… stuff."

"Wow." Eve was impressed despite his less than eloquent finish.

"You like that?" Ben asked. "I'm sure I contributed at least one thought to all the profoundness. Probably."

"I think you guys are deeper than we were giving you credit for. Some of the ladies were convinced you'd be discussing the value of rooting for a losing sports team because it makes the eventual victories sweeter."

"Well, that's a good answer, too. I'm not giving up on my Angels."

Eve laughed. He still followed a local team he'd helped coach in high school even though it had different kids every year. His dad sponsored them with his realty logo on the t-shirts. "I thought of you when we – I mean, you and your dad and your brother – during the first question because several people mentioned home as a significant place and you guys make homes. You make them better anyway."

"Uh…. we don't *make* anything," he said. "We improve houses, but we leave them empty. The furniture and the people make them into homes."

"That's true." Eve smiled at the sweet sentiment. "How do you know what to do to improve a house?"

"It's usually pretty obvious by the stains on the carpet or the rotting wood or the… you know, toilet that flushes into the nearby creek instead of the sewer system. Nate had a field day with that one."

"You already resold that one, didn't you?"

"Yeah. That one we've been redoing over near Vermillion is ready to go on the market, and we don't close on the one in Perrysburg until next week. I'm going to have more free time than usual this week."

Thinking about how he might like to spend that time made Eve nervous. She needed to wrap up the conversation. "It'll be nice for you to get some rest, and I have to work next Friday so I'm glad that means you'll be able to tell me about that meeting."

The pause could mean he believed she'd missed the hint. She wasn't sure.

"I'm always happy to talk to you about the other, secret half of the meetings, too," he said.

She smiled. Ben had joked before about how he liked having an inside source for the discussions he missed. Given that about half the ladies were dating or married to about half the guys, there were a lot of inside sources. "Okay," Eve said. "I'll look forward to next Friday, and you can look forward to the Friday after that when I might not have to work."

"Good plans usually involve the word *might*," he teased. "Have a good night, Eve."

"Bye." She hung up feeling disappointed. They usually talked longer, but that had felt like the appropriate end. She rushed the phone downstairs to the charger to remove the temptation to look at it again before bed. She sighed as she returned to her bible because she knew she wasn't going to focus on it. Drew and Aiden would be home for Christmas break in a month. Why did it seem the time was getting longer rather than shorter?

2

Anna dropped off her toddler shortly after Eve finished breakfast the next morning. She had to settle for a peek at the infant since she was sound asleep in her carrier. Maybe she'd be awake when Anna returned, and Eve could hold her then.

Anna handed Eve a diaper bag and quickly slipped out the door. She felt that the longer she lingered, the more likely Spencer would cry when she left. Eve scooped him up and placed him on her hip. She grabbed a stuffed dog with her free hand and pretended it was talking to distract the little guy from his mom's disappearance.

"Hello, Spencer. How are you today?"

"That's not what dogs say." Matt walked over and snatched the stuffed animal from Eve. He wiggled it against Spencer's neck while he said, "They say woof. Woof! Woof! Woof!"

Spencer giggled, and his adorable laugh was contagious.

Matt handed the dog back and walked away, apparently content to have shown himself the superior entertainer.

Eve's parents were at the church, and she didn't know where James was. That didn't matter since he wasn't two. She set Spencer down and followed him around the house for a while, naming whatever he pointed at. The kid knew quite a few words, but he mostly communicated by pointing.

He discovered a decorative cloth on the coffee table, which he pulled off and handed to Eve. Watching her spread and smooth it out again was so fun he handed it to her at least ten more times. After fifteen minutes of that, Eve decided it was time for their outing. She put Spencer's coat back on and grabbed her own. She considered stuffing her purse into the diaper bag but figured there was no need to make it heavier for a short walk. She slung the strap over her head. She told Matt where they were going because her parents would probably be back first and ask, then she took Spencer's hand to head to the library.

It was a long walk despite the short distance. That was only partly because toddlers have tiny legs. Mostly, it was because he needed to point at every single crack in the sidewalk. And he didn't just point. He needed to reach down and touch his finger to the ground so Eve knew exactly where he was pointing. He kept making a K sound, which Eve interpreted as attempts to say the word crack. She just kept telling him over and over that he was absolutely brilliant for recognizing all those cracks.

With the library in sight, Eve decided that she wasn't losing patience if she picked him up. She was cold, and a good babysitter would make sure her charge wasn't outside long enough to get cold. He felt warm in her arms though. Maybe she wouldn't be cold if she'd been doing a squat every few feet.

Spencer let himself be carried until they got inside the library, and then he wiggled to be set down again. Eve kept a firm grip on his hand to keep a proper indoor pace. The little boy led her up and down rows of shelves almost as though he knew where he was going. The path was too meandering to be fully convincing. He

17

came out the end of a row and started tugging hard past the next several. Eve looked ahead to determine what he'd spotted.

Ben Shannon was sitting in a big armchair with a book. Spencer appeared to be headed directly for him. Why was Spencer pulling her towards Ben?

Eve's mind scrambled to process what was happening while her body did nothing to stop it. Ben looked up and smiled in surprise at the same moment that Eve realized he wasn't Spencer's target after all. It was the empty chair next to Ben. Eve let him have both hands to climb onto the giant – to him – chair.

"Hi," Ben said softly. They were in a library. "Is this your nephew?"

"Yeah. This is Spencer."

"Hi, Spencer."

The kid finished his climb and sat up just long enough to look very pleased with himself. Then he flipped onto his stomach so he could wiggle his feet back to the floor.

"What's your oldest brother's name again?" Ben asked.

"John."

"Right. And he and his wife just had a second baby, right?"

"Yeah." Eve put a hand near Spencer's back to make sure he didn't fall as he hit the ground. He stumbled just one step before he got his balance and launched himself at the chair for another climb. Eve was slightly distracted wondering how long this game would last and also trying not to hope it would keep Spencer busy as it gave her time to talk with Ben. "They had a little girl a few weeks ago. She's so tiny she makes Spencer look big."

Ben smiled at the thought as he watched the toddler sit against the back of the chair with his feet not even reaching the end of the seat. That lasted another two seconds before Spencer flipped to slide down again.

"What are you reading?" She gestured to the book he'd set aside when she arrived.

"*Five Kingdoms*," he said. "It's a series I read several years ago. I thought I'd see if it's still as good as I remember."

"Is it?"

"I'm only a few chapters in."

Eve steadied Spencer as he touched the ground again. She and Ben shared a smile as he began to scramble back into the chair.

"Are you going to get him some books while you're here?"

"I don't think he'll sit still long enough for a book," Eve said, "but I hope to find something for me."

"Do you read a lot?"

"Not as much as I used to," she said. "I decided a little over a year ago that I wanted to get serious about reading the entire bible so I told myself that was what I had to pick up whenever I wanted to read. It's mostly made me read less of everything else so I'm thinking of revisiting that plan. But I have made some progress. I've read at least a third of it."

"That might be more than me," Ben admitted. "What are you getting today?"

"Nonfiction with lots of pictures so it won't really count as reading if I pick it up instead of a bible, but that's not why I need it."

He wrinkled his eyes and repeated, "Nonfiction with pictures? Do you have something specific in mind?"

"Only the subject. Something on interior design," she clarified.

Spencer turned away from the chair, and Eve grabbed his hand as he seemed ready to explore more. "I guess it's time to find out where that section is."

Ben followed her without words to search the catalog. It felt natural, comfortable. Did their friendship make it happen or had something in Eve's manner expressly invited him to tag along? Was she overthinking something innocent? Maybe it was best to focus on the moment. It was hard enough to type left-handed while slightly bent to hang on to a toddler without adding mental gymnastics. She checked the call number for the first book on the subject, knowing similar ones would be nearby. "747," she said. Then she let Spencer drag her into the 200s.

"I'm not sure the person who can't count should be leading," Ben said.

"We'll get there eventually."

Spencer got to the end of the row and turned the right way but he walked past so many rows he just skipped the one they needed.

"Are you sure he'll get us there?" Ben asked.

"The sooner I pick up a book, the sooner I have to carry it around. It might be better to get it right before we leave anyway."

Spencer found a book facing out on the bottom shelf. "Boo! Boo!" he said while poking it.

"That's right. It's blue." Most of the cover was blue anyway.

"He knows colors already?" Ben sounded impressed.

"I'm not sure," Eve admitted. "He might have said book now that I think about it. I just try to sound encouraging to whatever he says because he seems to talk a lot more when Anna or John is around. This one's yellow." She pointed at another cover facing out.

Spencer pointed at it and said something that sounded a little like yellow. Eve didn't know if he understood the color or was only copying the word she said. They seemed to have found a sports section because the next book to catch her eye had several balls on the cover, which was a word she knew Spencer knew.

"Look, Spencer. There's a ball."

"Ball!" He pointed and said it more clearly than most of his words.

When he kept saying it, Eve realized that he was trying to point out all of the balls on the cover. They were a shelf too high for him to touch. She touched each one for him as he proudly identified them all as balls.

Ben pulled a few books from a higher shelf. He sat on the floor in front of Spencer and used the pictures on the covers to begin to explain the differences between a baseball, a basketball, a soccer ball and a tennis ball. He probably explained a few others, but Eve was paying less attention than the toddler, who appeared fully engrossed and kept pointing at pictures to get Ben to keep talking about them.

The scene in front of Eve was troubling, and not because of her lack of interest in the number of hexagons on a soccer ball or how much bigger a softball was than a baseball. Watching Ben entertain her young nephew touched a mushy spot on her heart, a spot that Eve didn't want to acknowledge. "I don't think he's the one slowing me down now," she said.

Ben smiled sheepishly up at her. Then he spoke directly to Spencer for her to overhear. "We're going to have to continue our sports talk later," he said. "Your aunt wants to look at decorating books?" He wrinkled his face in exaggerated confusion.

Spencer giggled.

Eve bent to pick up the toddler while Ben collected the books. But Spencer didn't want to be carried. At least, he didn't want to be carried by Eve. He jumped in Ben's lap and grabbed the front of his shirt. Eve didn't feel slighted. With all her brothers, she was used to the guys in her life preferring the company of other guys. And the startled expression on Ben's face was too funny not to smile.

"I guess I'll get the books," she said. She watched Ben while she picked them up, watched the way he seemed uncertain how to get to his feet holding a toddler, like maybe it was something he'd never done before. Yet he didn't struggle or seem unhappy about it.

He smiled at Eve with a tiny nod that indicated he and Spencer were ready to follow her.

Eve dropped the extra books on a reshelving cart, hanging on to the one Ben had been reading. She moved straight to the subject number she was glad was easy to remember despite the sports detour. The first book she saw was called *Fabulous Dining Rooms*. She laughed at how absolutely unhelpful that would be in turning her dining room into anything else. But chair was another word she knew Spencer knew well so she pulled it down anyway.

She opened it and let him point to some chairs while her eyes scanned nearby titles. There was something with a title about the needs of all types of rooms. That was vague enough to be promising. Eve swapped that for the book on chairs. She flipped through it just enough to confirm it was full of pictures. That was enough to decide it was what she wanted, though she still doubted it would help.

"This'll be… oh, no. I didn't bring my library card." Eve's mind flashed to the purse she'd thought she wouldn't need still on a hook at her house.

"You can use my card," Ben said. "I assume I can trust you not to steal that book." He cast his eyes suspiciously over her, which made her feel something other than suspicious.

"Oh, um… I'm sure if I just give my name at the desk that'll work."

"That's no fun." Ben started walking. "Spencer wants to use the self-checkout."

Eve had no choice but to follow. "How do you know that's what he wants? I don't think he even knows what that is."

"Are you kidding? You push buttons and make it beep. I'm willing to bet *you* want to do that. There's no way a little kid doesn't."

That was an irrefutable argument, once the little kid was made aware of the buttons and beeps. It appeared they were going to make him aware as Ben led the way to the station. He handed the scanner to Spencer while he pulled a library card out of his pocket, then helped him aim at the barcode on the back. It took several tries to get it to register, but it made a different lower-pitched beep when it scanned nothing, and that was just as satisfactory to the toddler.

Eve held up her book for Spencer to scan. Ben pointed where he should aim and let him click it several times before they got the right beep. "Now this one," Eve said, holding up Ben's book.

"I already… Well, let's find out what happens if you scan something that's already checked out."

Spencer got it on the first try. The screen flashed a message that told them what they already knew. Ben encouraged him to scan it a few more times anyway. It wasn't clear who was having more fun. Eve used the time to stuff her book into the diaper bag so she'd have both hands free to take her nephew back when he finished playing with the scanner. Despite his earlier protest, he came willingly into Eve's arms while Ben got the self-checkout ready for the next person.

She thanked Ben and promised not to lose the book on his card. He left the library at the same time, telling her he was looking forward to the next Friday meeting before splitting off to the parking lot while Eve and Spencer stayed on the sidewalk. The kid wanted to walk again at the same time Ben's car went past. That worked out well for Eve because she was too busy setting him down and getting a good grip on his hand to pay attention to whether or not Ben had looked at her or waved at her or anything else she didn't want to know. The trip had already unsettled her.

Ben had evidently checked out a library book and then sat reading it only until Eve bumped into him. She didn't want to think about how much coincidence played into the morning. She hadn't told Ben she was going to the library, but she'd told Tori while he was only a few feet away.

Spencer gave her somewhere else to focus her attention. He was no longer interested in the cracks in the sidewalk. The grass needed a lot of pointing though. About halfway home, they passed someone walking a dog. Spencer knew the word doggy, and he said it at least ten times while Eve assured him that he was correct. She hoped he was only identifying it and not saying he wanted to go after it.

They were walking up the porch steps – a slow process when each step was nearly as high as one person's knees – when her parents pulled into the garage. She didn't notice either of them even looking her way as they moved from the garage to the back

24

door. Her parents didn't fuss over grandchildren the way some people seemed to.

Spencer let go of her hand as soon as she opened the door, and she let him run inside.

Matt yelled, "Incoming!" Then he squatted to let Spencer barrel into him and appear to knock him over.

While they were disentangling and getting off the floor, Eve's mom asked if she found anything at the library.

"Just one book." She dropped the diaper bag to retrieve that book before she forgot. She squashed an impulse to mention running into Ben. It wasn't important enough to mention, or else she hoped not mentioning it would make it unimportant. "It has a lot of pictures so I'm hoping something will inspire me."

James snorted. "But if you actually do something with that room, you'll lose your favorite hobby of dreaming about what to do with the room."

"It's not a hobby," Eve said. "I just can't decide."

Her brother knew that, and they both knew he'd been teasing. He smiled smugly at having provoked a reaction.

Eve spent some time playing with Spencer and getting him some lunch before his mom returned. Anna didn't stay long because it was nearly naptime for her toddler. She enjoyed hearing how cute he was on the trip to the library, though it felt even more deliberate when Eve left Ben out of her descriptions. After closing the door behind Anna and her kids, Eve returned to her unfinished room. Her notebook remained empty as she had no ideas. The new book, it turned out, had a ton of pictures of ideas she didn't like.

*D*an was frowning at Eve when she entered the restaurant Wednesday morning, though 11am was hardly morning anymore. It had taken her a minute to get the front door unlocked. It almost looked as though he'd spent that minute perfecting his intimidating stare. Fortunately, her boss was also her uncle. That made him less scary.

"Tell everyone I said no," Dan said.

"You want to kill the Christmas pizza?" She batted her eyes to make sure he saw how that would be disappointing.

"I'm not killing the Christmas pizza," he said. "Don't look at me like I'm King Herod or something. We just need to kill the speculation that we might auction off one of Noah's overly complicated disasters. I don't believe anyone would pay a hundred dollars for that anyway, let alone two thousand."

Apparently, he'd been reading the comments. "It's only November," Eve said. "We could probably let it die on its own."

"Tell everyone I said no," he repeated. "And don't embellish it or exaggerate it. I don't want my head on the Grinch's body or any other cartoon. Just a plain and simple no."

"Yes, sir," Eve said, scurrying into the kitchen. "As soon as I get home tonight." She smiled when he grunted at her tiny victory. They both knew she wasn't supposed to do any of the social stuff during her regular work hours.

Eve liked her job. Working in a small-town pizza place didn't have glamour or prestige, but it was low-stress and the only work she ever took home involved stirring up fun conversations online and occasionally roasting her coworkers. She took a few orders for Franks' Pizza early, which would make Noah happy when he came in later. Franks' Pizza was his idea. It was a special that came with a bouquet of Sarah Franks' flowers. They sold a limited number of them every Wednesday evening. Though they rarely received requests after they hit the limit, the perceived scarcity made customers want to get in their requests early.

Noah came in only an hour before Eve would leave for the day. She watched him when one of the drivers told him most of the Franks' Pizzas had already been ordered. He nodded with satisfaction. That was not surprising. The only thing surprising was that Eve had expected his reaction to reveal whether or not he and Sarah were officially together. She did get another chance to pry a short time later when he approached her.

"Hey, Eve," Noah said. "Do you have plans for tomorrow?"

"Uh. No, not really."

"I was thinking that if you wanted to switch, you can work tomorrow and I'll take Friday so you can go to St. Jude's."

"Now that you can see Sarah whenever you want, you don't need to make sure you get those few minutes before the meetings on Fridays?" she asked.

Noah smiled at her, not in a way that confirmed anything, only in a way that said he was happy to know something she didn't.

27

But then he turned serious. "Actually, it was pointed out to me recently that it's rather selfish of me to take every Friday off when you might enjoy those meetings as much as I do."

"Hmm." Eve didn't know how to respond to the offer. Noah had already been taking every Friday off when she started there, and it hadn't occurred to her that there might be anything unfair about it.

"I sometimes forget you qualify as an adult now," he said.

"I'm only four years younger than you."

He shrugged. "You can say only now, but it used to... I finished high school before you even started. You were a kid to me for a long time."

Eve considered her brothers, the ones who were three and five years younger than her and still in high school. Noah had a good point. She did not admit that to her cousin. She simply thanked him and agreed to trade shifts. Then she asked if he was planning to spend some of his new day off with Sarah.

"I'll probably find some time to brainstorm a New Year's pizza." He clearly said it as much to watch his dad shake his head as to deflect the question about Sarah.

Eve laughed at both of them.

When she got home after work, she went straight to the dining room that wasn't a dining room. It was completely empty except for the notebook that had been on her lap the last time she failed to be inspired and the library book that failed to give inspiration. She sat on the floor with her back against the wall. The notebook stayed on the carpet as there was no reason to record her lack of ideas. The book stayed on the carpet as there was no reason to believe it would be better a second time.

First, Eve did have some work to finish. She typed out a message to her followers that Dan was not going to auction anything. She said they would have to imagine his head on the Grinch because she wasn't allowed to post that. Someone would take the hint and share the image for her. Dan would laugh. He might refuse to laugh in front of anyone, but he would laugh. He wasn't as curmudgeonly as he liked to project. She made a note that a rumor of a New Year's pizza could be her next teaser. Then she put her phone down to focus on the room.

It had one entrance that was a wide archway and a big window on the opposite wall. It was a blank canvas. Eve's mind painted nothing. Again. It was time to ask for help. Eve decided to text Grandpa Will first. His response was bound to be amusing even if it wasn't helpful. She sent him a message asking what he'd want to do with an extra room in his house.

She called Aiden while she waited for a response.

"Hi, Eve. I guess it's Wednesday again."

She called him every Wednesday, and that was almost always how he answered.

"I have a question for you," she said. "If you had an extra room to design, what would you turn it into?"

"Have you still not decided what to do with Simon's room?"

"There are too many options."

"What options have you considered so far?" he asked.

"Um… nothing."

He laughed. "How many options is nothing?"

Eve laughed with him. "That's my problem. I feel like this room could be anything. And yet I can't actually think of anything to do with it."

"Hmm. Well, you know I live in a dorm that's basically my bedroom and my living room and my dining room and... if I had an extra room, I'd probably want it to stay empty so I could stretch out."

"I guess you'll be glad to be home for a while."

"Yeah. The break will be nice." Aiden updated her on some of his classes, including a group project that was going surprisingly well and a paper with a looming due date. By the time they hung up, Grandpa Will had responded.

Eve smiled at the message before she even understood it. Grandpa Will's eyesight wasn't great, and he liked to put more space than normal between the words he typed to make them easier to read. Though there were usually enough misspellings and repeated letters to suggest he didn't really read what he sent.

This text included a word spelled nrrrd. Eve didn't think he was calling her a nerd. That didn't sound like him. The message started with if with an extra i and the word you was clear. Oh, need. E was next to r. Eve decided he was telling her that if she didn't know what to do with something, then she didn't need it. That *did* sound like him. Grandpa Will was always going off on the dangers of excess.

She thanked him for the advice. While it wasn't directly helpful, she would try to remember not to fill the room with anything useless, assuming she ever decided what would be useful.

Eve wanted to call Ben next. He spent so much time remodeling that he might have an idea. He was an electrician though, and she was pretty sure there wouldn't be any rewiring involved in her project. Even more importantly, she knew she didn't want to talk to him for expertise but simply because she wanted to talk to him. She dialed Drew instead.

The voicemail was predictable. He rarely answered his phone. "Hi, Drew," she said. "I'm still trying to figure out what to do with Simon's old music room. Give me a call if you have any brilliant ideas." She dropped her phone on top of her notebook and got up to pace the room.

The movement didn't help. It didn't help her see anything but a blank slate. And it didn't remove her temptation. She returned to her spot on the carpet and called Ben.

"Eve?" He sounded a little surprised but not upset.

"You're not busy now?"

"Told you it'd be a quiet week. I've mostly been home since lunch."

"Oh."

"I guess you're not working tonight either?" he asked.

"Yeah. I opened. Noah traded shifts with me while I was there," she said. That could be the reason she thought to call Ben. "I'm going to work tomorrow instead of Friday so you won't have to take detailed notes for me or anything and I can share the ladies' side with you."

"Nice. Since I normally take detailed notes." The light sarcasm meant he appreciated her joke.

Eve smiled as she pictured Ben smiling. "I'm also calling because I need some help."

"With what?"

"I'm trying to turn a dining room into something that's not a dining room, and I don't know what to do."

"Uh... I'm not sure I followed that."

"I'll start at the beginning. You know my brother Simon is a musician, right? He writes songs and everything."

"Yeah." He only said the one word, but she heard him wanting to ask what that had to do with dining rooms.

"There's this room in our house that's supposed to be a formal dining room. But we have a good size kitchen, and we just always eat in there. My mom made this a playroom when we were all really little. Then she let Simon turn it into, uh, I guess he liked to call it a studio when he was a teenager. He kept instruments in here. I'm sitting in it right now. And he added some kind of sound panels to the walls and did all his practicing here. Anyway, when he moved out a few months ago, my mom told me I could do whatever I want with it. I don't know if that's because I'm the oldest one still living here full time or because I'm the only girl. She did say I could make it as girly as I wanted. But now I have this room I can use however I want. Every now and then I look at it and think about how it should look... And all I can think is how do I make a dining room look like something else and that makes me see dining room and nothing else."

"Uh... well, I don't think I can help you make it girly," Ben said.

"It doesn't have to be," Eve said. "I just thought... you see more houses than I do. Maybe you've seen an interesting room somewhere."

"Hmm. I have seen some interesting things. But it's not usually the good kind of interesting. More like the I can't believe they didn't burn the house down with this creative wiring kind of interesting."

Eve made sure he could hear her laugh through the phone. "I don't think I'm going to do anything electrical. But even the bad kind of interesting might spark an idea."

"Was that a pun?" He seemed to be trying not to groan.

32

"What? Oh. Spark an idea. That wasn't intentional."

"Okay. If you say so."

"It wasn't," Eve insisted. "I bet you've used that one before to have picked up on it so fast."

"No comment."

"So anyway, have you seen any… I don't know… nontraditional uses of rooms? Something that wasn't a basic living room or dining room?"

"Uh…" He stretched the one syllable out while he thought. "I don't think so. The houses we buy are usually cleared out. I can't really tell what most of the rooms were for. People do paint things unusual colors though. A dark gray room comes to mind. Someone had painted a mural of a fish tank in one room."

"I guess you sell them unfurnished, too, don't you?"

"Yeah. We intentionally make everything as neutral as possible so potential buyers can picture it however they want."

Eve brightened. "Oh. Have you ever had anyone walking through a house say something like… I don't know… this'll be a great space for our… uh… you see how I have no ideas?"

Ben seemed amused by her frustration. "I'm sorry. My dad does all the selling."

"I think you're just really determined not to help me."

"Well… what do *you* want to use this room for?"

"I don't know." Eve sighed loudly at him. "Have you not been listening this whole time. I have no ideas."

"I think you have a lot of good ideas," Ben said. His tone got more serious, like he suddenly wasn't talking about her dining room problem.

Eve tensed. They needed to keep the conversation light and

innocent. "Apparently, calling you for inspiration wasn't one of them."

"Ouch," he said. "I guess if I had an extra room, I'd want to see what it naturally turned into."

"What do you mean?"

"I think if you spend time in the room, you'll start thinking things like... I wish I had a better place to sit. I wish my... whatever was in here. The window should let in more light. Things like that."

"That's not bad," Eve admitted. "Maybe I am trying too hard to get to a finished product and should think smaller. My grandpa said if I didn't know what to do with something, then I don't need it. I think you're saying kind of the same thing. Wait and see what I need."

"Maybe. But when you do decide, let me know if you need help moving things or painting or something. I'm better with hands on help than, you know, ideas."

Eve loved the idea of painting the room with Ben. She needed to hang up. "Okay. I'm going to keep thinking. I'll see you Friday." She set the phone down as quickly as she could. A surge of nerves made her stand up again. She examined the room. What was one thing it needed? The walls had a lot of scuffs and holes where Simon had taken stuff down. It needed paint. Maybe a color was her starting point.

When she tried to picture a color, all she could see was Ben with a paintbrush, smiling approval at whatever color she'd chosen. She imagined him reaching across the window with a tape measure, shaking his head slightly to get his dark hair out of his eyes. She imagined him pulling a hammer from a tool belt. Why he would need a hammer to repair holes was beyond her, but her mind seemed to like the manly tool in his hand.

Her phone lit up with a welcome distraction. Unfortunately, it was a two-word response from Drew. "Man cave."

She rolled her eyes and decided she was done with that room for the night.

4

*E*ve pulled the headband off hard enough that it stretched and snapped back on her fingers. Fortunately, the fabric was very soft. She set it on the counter and used both hands to smooth down her brown hair. It was super straight, and she never would have guessed getting it to lay flat would be a problem. She was trying to grow out some bangs though and used headbands to hold them back. They'd gotten to the length that if she put the headband on wrong, little fringe would pop out behind her ears. She picked up the pink headband to try again.

She groaned and tried a third time. On the fourth attempt, her hair stayed down. She vowed to remember this stage if she was ever tempted to snip bangs again.

Eve skipped down the stairs, her mood surprisingly light considering the uncooperative hair. Both of her parents were sitting on the couch.

"Off to St. Jude's?" her mom asked.

Eve nodded. "Where are the boys?"

"They went to the park to shoot hoops with some friends."

"It's barely above freezing," Eve said.

Her dad shrugged at her. "They'll be running around. And it's not like they'd prefer whatever we're going to land on here." He was moving from picture to picture with the remote, having apparently not decided which movie they were going to watch. Her parents enjoyed watching cheesy romances they spent the whole time picking apart. Eve liked to join them. Matt and James didn't appreciate people talking during movies, either those watching or those in the movie. They preferred scenes where stuff was exploding or at least on the verge of exploding.

"You guys can tell me about it later," Eve said.

"Pink is a nice color on you, by the way." Her mom smiled approvingly.

"Thanks." Eve dashed towards the door before anyone asked if she dressed up for anyone in particular. Not that her parents would ask that. Why would they? Eve had simply made a little more effort than usual with her long wool skirt and pink sweater because she didn't have to go almost straight from work. If anyone happened to notice she looked nice, including her mom, it didn't mean anything.

Eve turned on the heater in her car even though she knew it wouldn't warm up before she got to the church. A couple of young women she didn't know well were rushing towards the door just ahead of her and one waited to hold the door for her. She smiled her thanks and followed them towards the music room.

The toddlers were still being set up in the hall. Eve claimed a chair by putting her coat on the back of it. She straightened her sweater as she sat to watch the others arriving. Ben Shannon came in almost as soon as her eyes faced the door. He wore a black coat and something else black was wadded up in his hand. He smiled when he saw her, which made her heart stutter. As he moved to

37

take the seat next to her, she noticed his hair was darker and shinier than usual.

"Is your hair wet?" she asked.

"We pulled out some really old carpet today," he said. "I needed a shower."

"Are you trying to freeze to death going outside like that?"

He unwadded the black thing to show her a hat. "That's what this is for. To not freeze to death."

Eve didn't blush easily, but she felt a bit of embarrassment at not recognizing a hat. In her defense, his hair didn't look as though it'd been recently plastered to his head. It still bounced lightly off his forehead. She had also been distracted from anything in his hand by the way his eyes seemed to light up at the sight of her. There was no way she could voice her defense. She said only, "Good idea."

"Have you had any ideas?" He unzipped his coat but left it on. "About the room you told me about?"

"Sort of. I still don't really know, but… I'm going to take your advice and do one thing at a time."

He nodded. "Have you decided on a first thing?"

"Paint," she said. "The walls are scuffed and marked up from Simon's stuff. I think I'll want to paint it no matter what else I do so I'm going to start there. I bought paint this afternoon." She smiled, feeling oddly proud of having bought a can of paint.

"What color?" Ben asked.

"I found a shade called Cheerful Yellow. I thought that sounded pretty cheerful."

"Definitely. Did you start painting this afternoon, too?"

Eve shook her head. "I didn't get back with the paint until

almost dinner, and… I want to try to do it all at once. How long will it take me?"

"Depends on the size of the room, and…" Ben paused to smile a greeting at Cassidy and Sarah as they sat on Eve's other side. "Also depends on prep work and stuff. You said the room is empty but the walls are marked up. Do they need patching?"

Eve shrugged because she did not know the answer to the question. "I'm going to paint a room in my house," she said to get Cassidy caught up.

"Make sure you have good ventilation," Cassidy said. "It takes forever for the smell to fade."

Ben nodded at that advice.

Eve wondered how she'd accomplish that without inviting winter into the room.

"If you want help…" Ben glanced around the room nervously. "We do have a ton of supplies. If I brought over rollers and drop cloths, we could probably have it done in an hour. Or somewhere close to an hour. And I have plaster if it does need patching."

"I…" Eve really wanted his help. Ben had a lot more experience, meaning in this case more than none. He apparently knew how to patch walls when she didn't even know how to tell if they needed it. But she didn't want him to take over. "I bought a brush," she said. "When I pictured painting the room, I pictured a paintbrush. I don't know why, but now I want that experience."

"Yes!" Cassidy sucked in an excited breath. "We were just talking last week about how we choose to invest time in things that are important and how we make things important with the time we invest."

Ben smiled at the connection. "Okay. Brushes will take longer," he looked at Eve and gestured at Cassidy, "but if you don't want to rush an experience... Do you want me to help at all?"

"Are you free Sunday afternoon?"

"Yes."

Eve's stomach swooshed at how quickly he agreed to something that was only supposed to be a practical working arrangement. "Bring a brush for you and the things I don't know I need, maybe about 2 o'clock. Do you know where I live?"

"Yeah. I had to pick up stuff from your mom a few... uh..." Ben's hands froze on the hat he'd been tossing back and forth as a wary expression landed on his face. "Is your mom recruiting volunteers for anything right now?"

Eve laughed at the familiar reaction to thoughts of her mom. "She's *always* recruiting someone for something, but don't worry. I'll run interference."

Sarah leaned over Cassidy. "Wait. Are you the one person in the parish who can actually say no to Mrs. Donnolly?"

"Sort of. I can't say no when she asks as my mom because... she's my *mom*. But when she asks me something as Mrs. Donnolly, chief of church volunteers, then I can say no because she's not asking as my mom."

"Interesting paradox," Cassidy said.

"Sunday 2 pm," Ben confirmed as he stood up. He gave his chair to Heather, who had arrived while Eve wasn't paying attention to the room filling up. He went to join a few guys standing by the door. Eve was only aware of that out of the corner of her eye. Her primary attention was on Gabriel and Ruth and whether or not they were about to start the meeting. At least, that was where her

40

attention was outwardly. Her appearance should convey that she was calm and not overly excited about anything.

Gabriel flipped open his notebook. Eve relaxed with real focus as he said a prayer for a fruitful conversation before taking the guys out of the room with him.

Ruth smiled at all of the ladies as they settled into a circle. "We're continuing the theme from last week," she said, "the theme of saints who aren't officially called saints with a capital S. We're going to talk about Judas Maccabeus from, rather obviously, the book of Maccabees. He helped with the rededication of the temple, and last week we talked about the re*building* of the temple so that's why it's sort of a continuation." She winced apologetically as she looked down at her notes.

Ruth sometimes seemed concerned about being unqualified to lead the group. But Eve appreciated her humility. She appreciated that Ruth tried to share a few facts, and then presented open-ended questions. Eve usually learned something each week and also went away with a deep thought to think, which was an opportunity for growth beyond simple facts.

"I know everyone has read the entire Old Testament," Ruth continued lightly, "but here's a quick recap in case Maccabees has been awhile. Judas Maccabeus and his family lived at a time when pagans had taken over the Jewish temple. They led a revolt to reclaim the temple for God. When it was rededicated, they celebrated for eight days, which is where Hanukah started. Judas Maccabeus resisted pressure – hostile violent pressure – to worship the false gods. We're lucky to live in a time and place where violence is rarely involved, but when have you felt pressure to turn your back on God? Or have you seen others experience that kind of pressure?"

"I guess we're not really going with an icebreaker today, huh?" Tori observed.

"Yeah, it's a… This could be overly personal," Ruth said. "That's why I included the part about seeing pressure to turn from God more in society in general."

"I can answer personally, mostly because some of the people here already know this about me." Heather's eyes bounced around the room taking note of those people. "I was raised in the Church. But when I was in college, I became friends with a few girls who were not. They laughed at me for going to church every Sunday, made me feel like I was absurd for even believing in God. I guess my faith wasn't very strong because I found it easy to choose my friends," she paused for air quotes, "over God. I spent a few years trying to win their approval and became someone I didn't like. Through a long story I won't go into, I actually started coming to this group before I started going back to church. I met some great people who followed Christ, became real friends to me, and gave me the courage to admit I missed God."

"He missed you, too," Emily said.

A few others nodded and smiled encouragingly. The room was silent for a few heartbeats. No one seemed to want to move on too quickly from something that might have been difficult to share.

"Well…" Brianna started slowly. "One small way that I turned my back on God was praying before meals. I was very diligent about thanking God until sometime in high school when I started hiding it. If anyone outside my family was around, I'd pray silently and avoid the visual Sign of the Cross. And then I realized I got in the habit of skipping the prayer altogether."

"I skipped the prayer during school lunches, too," Emily admitted.

"Me, too."

"I skipped the Sign of the Cross," Jessica said. "And I went to a Catholic high school. I saw very few other kids doing it, and they got teased for being holier-than-thou."

Eve was comforted in having company in that particular failing. But she was also forced to realize she usually forgot to thank God when she ate without others around to remind her.

"I have to admit," Brianna said, "even now when I go out in public – like a restaurant – I might not have the guts to flaunt an obvious prayer if my husband wasn't there doing it with me."

Strength in numbers underscored the next few examples, friends who advocated poor choices and how much easier it was to do the right thing when another person had your back. Yet all the while, the knowledge that God had your back should be enough. The discussion was weighty, but Ruth picked it up with her next question.

"After they reclaimed the temple, there was the eight-day celebration," she said. "If you were in charge of an eight-day celebration in honor of God, what would it be like?"

"Decorations," Eve said.

"What kind?"

"I'm not sure because I'm having trouble not picturing Christmas decorations. But I think pretty things help people feel like celebrating."

"And food," Heather said. "Like some kind of fancy dessert."

"Music." Emily wiggled in her chair as though she heard a fun beat.

"I'm on the fence about clothes," Sarah said. "I like picturing everyone all dressed up for the party, but nice clothes are not always the most comfortable. And for eight days…"

Emily stilled thoughtfully. "Yeah, eight days is a long time for something with the energy I'm picturing."

"I think eight days leaves room for a lot of different activities and… moods."

"I agree. It should be more like a series of events."

"Yes!" Heather sat up straighter as she spread her hands. "It could start with a solemn day, one that maybe involves ritual preparations, adding decorations a little at a time. Each day would be a little more… festive, until the big high-energy party on the last day."

Eve nodded along with that plan, then Jessica described something somewhat opposite that started with a big blowout and gradually wound down. Eve thought that could work, too. The rest of the meeting was taken up with descriptions of potential decorations, which they agreed should be varying shades of purple and gold to symbolize the kingship of God.

It appeared the guys had wrapped up first. The room across the hall was already empty. A couple of the guys were helping clean up the kid area, and a few entered the music room to stack up all the chairs as the ladies were leaving.

Eve found that Ben was waiting outside for her. "Hey, Eve. Good discussion tonight?"

"Yeah."

"I'm gonna call you for details when you're home and warm," he said, "but as a teaser… us guys invented lasagna today."

Eve flashed a grin, mostly amused by his amusement, then rushed to her car. While she was curious now, hearing about it from inside a warm house felt like a good idea.

Her parents had finished the movie when she got home. They were describing it to her brothers, who seemed to enjoy being confused.

"She had to chose between ice sculpting and being an advertising exec."

"What?" Matt wrinkled his eyes at his mom.

"Apparently, this one weekend festival took as much time as a career."

"Did it pay as much as a full-time job?"

"I don't remember anyone really mentioning a prize."

"Was it… why was it important?"

"I think she liked it?" Eve's dad also seemed confused about what must have been a significant plot point.

Her mom shook her head. "She liked spending time with the guy who liked it. It was a two-person event. And since it was an annual thing, I don't know why she didn't just plan ahead to have that week off. But of course then there wouldn't be the drama about her possibly losing her job because of the time she spent on the practice sculptures."

"She was, like, skipping work?" James asked.

"I don't know."

"Yeah. It was never really clear whether her boss was being unreasonable and expecting too much or if she was missing set appointments or something."

"What I didn't get," Eve's dad tipped his head in an expression of concentration, "was how she – or the guy for that matter – learned how to ice sculpt in the first place. Am I forgetting some backstory?"

"No. I think we were just supposed to assume this was a natural skill they both had. Along with the fact that they had this amazing friendship based solely on having done the same event together the last two years."

"They didn't see each other otherwise?"

"Didn't sound like it. She was visiting her hometown for the festival, and remember at the beginning how her dad said he wished she had the time to visit more than once a year?"

"Oh, right. Why hadn't she taken time off for the thing?"

He got a shrug in response.

Eve felt her phone buzzing in her purse. She hadn't even taken off her coat. She shrugged out of it, then took her phone out of her purse before she hung both on the same hook. She answered as she climbed the stairs.

"Hi, Eve. You ready to talk?" Ben sounded hopeful.

"Almost," she said. "I got sucked into a conversation about a surprising amount of drama around making an ice sculpture."

"Did it fall or nearly crush someone?"

Eve smiled. "That sounds more interesting than what my parents were talking about." She shut her door, pushed her shoes off, and sat on the end of her bed. "Okay, now tell me about the lasagna."

"It was probably funnier at the time than being told about it," he started, "but we were addressing the question about what we'd want at an eight-day celebration. We agreed right away that food would be a highlight. Ryan said his mom made mac and cheese as a side for a lot of holiday meals, and he'd like to see that promoted to the main dish. Then someone said something about making sure it

46

wasn't ruined with ketchup, which I didn't know was a thing people did. Do people put ketchup on mac and cheese?"

"Not that I know personally," Eve said, "but some people seem to put ketchup on everything."

"Anyway, that got us talking about sauces that might be good instead. There was some consensus around a spicy red sauce. But Noah said it would be better layered so you could taste the red sauce and cheese sauce separately as you ate it. We were all thinking that sounded pretty good when Joseph was like, 'You guys know you're describing lasagna, right?'"

Eve laughed at the impression.

"I thought... layered noodles and cheese and sauce. That is pretty much lasagna, isn't it?"

"It does sound a little different."

"Good either way," Ben said.

"I do like lasagna."

"Yeah? So then we spent, I don't know, at least ten minutes discussing whether or not lasagna is actually a cross between mac and cheese and pizza. Someone was even trying to look up when each of those were invented. Gabriel got us back on topic before anything was decided."

"Huh." Eve considered the similarities. She liked breadsticks with lasagna, which was kind of like having the crust on the side. But pizza didn't have noodles. That could be how someone thought it merged with mac and cheese.

"It got me wondering if Noah might try to introduce a mac and cheese pizza next."

"I bet someone has already done that," Eve said, "but it wouldn't stop him from trying to do it better."

"Do you think he'd do it better?" Ben sounded genuinely interested in her opinion.

Eve took a moment to *not* appreciate that. "Yes. He has great ideas. They're just not always very practical. Or workable. I would have liked to try his inside out pizza."

"Inside out? I don't think I heard about that one."

"It was a while ago. He wanted to make a plain crust. I mean, still lightly seasoned, but no sauce, cheese or toppings. All of that would be in a ring around the crust. Then people could rip off pieces of crust and dip them in the toppings. He envisioned it as something very sharable, like a pizza appetizer."

"That could be good," Ben said. "Kind of like chips and dip only... not."

"Yeah. Except that pizza is already one of the most sharable foods, and the logistics of... It probably would have needed some sort of custom ring-shaped pan, and you can't just dump that into a pizza box so it wouldn't be available to carryout or delivery customers, which is a majority of the orders."

"You're right about it not being a practical idea."

"Dan was at his most sarcastic in nixing it. He was like, let's invest a lot of time and money to offer a fraction of our customers a pizza that looks like it fell apart and they have to put it back together before they can eat it."

Ben's laughter came through the phone before his words. "I'm sure there are people who would pay for the novelty of eating pizza differently, but I think I'd side with Dan on it not being worth the hassle for him."

"Sometimes I have to try really hard not to take sides."

"What do you mean? Is it difficult to stay out of the arguments at work?"

48

"Not at work." Eve thought about what she was trying to say. "It's never awkward. I think Dan and Noah have a great relationship where they both enjoy antagonizing each other, and they still make a great team. Some of Noah's ideas are kind of gimmicky, but they've been boosts for business. Dan appreciates that. And I think Noah appreciates that Dan keeps him in check, is better at seeing the potential pitfalls before they happen."

"Good." It was mostly a prompt to continue.

"What I meant was... my online persona... I try not to say what I personally think of anything. I actually try to present them both as morons when I see merit on both sides. That's tricky."

"Hmm." Ben might have been reviewing her posts in his mind. "You do seem to have a theme of... Noah wants to do this ridiculous thing and Dan is a tyrant for not allowing it."

"Yeah. Am I being too hard on them?"

"No. I think it's clear your comments are not mean-spirited. You're just, uh, stirring the pot in a fun way," Ben said. "Look at the way people respond. They comment with jokes, and they switch sides constantly. No one takes it seriously. And I bet the interest you generate helps Noah's ideas be good for business."

"Maybe." Ben's reassurance did help. Eve thought he had a good point about judging her posts by the way people reacted. No one had attacked Dan or Noah worse than sticking their heads in cartoons, or on the body of the Grinch. But she also realized that she and Ben had wandered from the topic of the meeting at church. That was why she was talking to him. "Getting back to where you invented lasagna as part of the celebration... I'm glad we got to talk about a party because the question before that was kind of hard."

"Uh... refresh my memory on what was right before that."

"The one about where we might feel pressure to turn our backs on God," Eve said. "A few of the ladies shared some personal things and... I don't know. It's just sometimes I feel like I'm not allowed to say anything when we talk about personal experience because I'm usually the youngest one in the room and therefore the least experienced."

"Just because you have less experience doesn't mean your experience is less valid," Ben said. Then he laughed. "I think I just quoted my dad, and we're not talking about electrical wiring but I think it still applied."

Eve smiled at the sentiment and the fact that it came from an unrelated type of experience.

"I think the guys got less personal on that one," Ben continued. "We mostly focused on people in general comparing our actions to the world's standards rather than God's. We think as long as we're better than average like, sure I've committed this sin and this sin but as long as I haven't done those way worse sins, then I'm fine because nobody's perfect. But we should instead be looking at where we fall short of God's standards. Just because we can't be perfect doesn't mean we can't be *better*."

"I like that," Eve said. "I mean, I like when I come away from a meeting with something to really ponder during the week so maybe this is where we should wrap it up so I can ponder being better."

"Okay. I guess I'll see you Sunday then."

Eve set the phone on her dresser and stared at its back while thoughts began to crowd into her head. They were thoughts about whether or not letting Ben help her paint a room was crossing a line. Would that help her be better or move her soul needle the other direction?

5

*E*ve pulled out a chair for Grandpa Will knowing what he was about to say.

"Oh, honey. You shouldn't have gone to so much trouble."

"It's soup and sandwiches, Dad." Eve's mom was his daughter. "I didn't exactly wear myself out putting this together."

"But they're toasted," he said. "Cold ham and cheese would have been just fine."

"Warm food is good on a cold day," Eve said.

"I didn't say I wasn't excited to eat this amazing meal." Grandpa Will folded his hands. "Let's thank the Good Lord for this bounty and the woman who skillfully put it together for us."

He didn't hear James snort at the word amazing. After the prayer, there were a few slurping sounds as people enjoyed the tomato soup. James ate his reluctantly. The table swelled on Sunday afternoons as Simon, Tori and Grandpa Will were regular guests after church.

"So… the Christmas Festival?"

"I said I'd take care of it, Mom," Simon said.

"What have you done so far?"

"If you want me to do it, maybe you should let me do it." Simon's tone was pointed but not belligerent. "You said you wanted a break this year. I'm not sure badgering me for details is much of a break."

Mrs. Donnolly sighed with an expression that grudgingly conceded his point. "I guess as long as I know Tori's helping you, I can try to let it go."

Tori was sitting next to Eve. Under her breath, she muttered, "I didn't *say* I would help him."

Eve returned the smile. Tori would help even if she hadn't been formally asked. And Eve would probably end up helping, too. The Christmas Festival was fun. She would make her brother ask for help though.

"Can I DJ?" Matt asked.

"Uh... probably." Simon reached for another sandwich from a platter in the center of the table. "Remind me you volunteered in a few weeks."

"In a few..."

Eve watched her mom concentrate on her spoonful of soup to stop herself from saying what she'd been about to say.

"This reminds me of the parking meters we used to have downtown," Grandpa Will said.

"What reminds you of parking meters, Dad? Talk of Christmas or that sandwich?"

"When you have ninety-one years of memories crowded in your head," he said, "everything will remind you of something, too."

Eve shared another smile with Tori. Grandpa Will was always launching into a random story sparked by a connection no one else could see.

"When we had those meters, we could get all our shopping done for a penny." He glanced around expecting disbelief.

James piped up. "You got groceries for a penny?"

"I didn't think you were *that* old," Matt said. He looked at his mom for clarification.

She shook her head. "Not the groceries," she said. "He means we only had to put a penny in the meter, and that's mostly true."

Eve waited for Grandpa Will to continue explaining.

"A penny got you twelve minutes," he said. "I'd get the list divided and the kids prepped before we got there. I'd give Dan the penny and he'd wait until the rest of us were at the door, then he'd stick it in the meter and run after us. Everyone had their assignments – your grandma made a very specific list – and we'd split up and meet back at the checkout."

"Mom would write down the brand and size of what she wanted, and how high the price could be before she expected you to skip it."

Grandpa Will nodded. "A *very* specific list. The boys could handle more items because they were older."

"Because they ran when they thought no one was looking."

"It never took longer than twelve minutes?" Matt asked.

Grandpa Will shook his head, but when he noticed his daughter nodding hers, he said, "Sometimes it was close. If the checkout was slow, I'd send one of the boys out with a spare penny. He'd know to stand by the meter and only use it if he spotted cops. Never had to use that extra penny."

Eve had a few thoughts on the story. She kept them to herself but might not have had a chance to share anyway. The parking meters reminded her grandpa of collecting tolls for the turnpike, a job he'd held for a few years once upon a time. Then an oddly painted truck he'd seen on that job reminded him of his first vegetable garden and how it grew carrots he didn't think he'd planted. Carrots reminded him of the time it rained on one of Dan's baseball games and the rain stopped again before the coaches could finish their argument over whether they should keep playing or call the game.

Everyone in the family was finished eating before he took a break in his storytelling. Eve liked hearing from him. She felt bad when she caught herself checking the time. Grandpa Will typically went home to nap after lunch. Simon would drive him. Tori didn't usually stay long once Simon left. Eve was wondering how many extra people might be in the house when Ben showed up to help her paint. She was also wondering if she'd chosen the time to make sure he didn't feel he was interrupting lunch or to limit the chances of extra people in the house. She wasn't trying to hide anything though. Her parents and two younger brothers already knew he was coming over.

Eve noticed her parents had begun to clear the table. Grandpa Will was looking at Simon.

"Well, Dan, are you ready to take me home? My eyelids are getting heavy."

"Simon," he corrected. "And yes, we can go now."

They both thanked everyone for the meal and the company. Eve gave her grandpa a gentle hug. He seemed somewhat frail in her arms. She simply waved at her brother. Then she went up to her room to change from church clothes into something she wouldn't be sad to accidentally ruin with paint. When she came down, Tori was still at the table with the rest of her family. Eve was pulled into a discussion about what game to play. She agreed to a

54

relatively short one, and the timing worked out that they were setting it up to play again without her when the doorbell rang.

Eve felt a twinge of disappointment when she opened the door to an empty porch.

"I'll be right there," Ben's voice called out.

She jumped, but it probably went unseen since he was busy pulling a bag out of the back of his truck. Looking down, Eve saw that the porch wasn't completely empty. There was a fan and a bucket of supplies. "Should I take these inside?" she asked.

He moved quickly and took the porch steps two at a time. "Yeah. I could have carried it all but I... I just forgot to grab this one."

As she closed the door behind them, Eve heard her mom's voice call out an answer she was certainly meant to hear. "She's going to bring him in here to say hello first."

She rolled her eyes. "I was already going to do that," she said so only Ben heard.

He smiled and followed her.

"I think you already know my parents and Matt, James, and Tori." She pointed to her brothers as she spoke. She was sure he knew her parents and Tori and her brothers' names. But it was possible he didn't know which was which. All the Donnollys had hair in varying shades of brown and the youngest two had basically the same cut. Matt wore glasses, plain metal frames but still the most differentiating thing from his brother.

"Hi, everyone," Ben said with a nod. "Sorry about the paint fumes we're about to unleash. I brought a fan to vent some, but... uh... yeah... It's gonna smell like paint."

"It will smell like work." Eve's mom smiled at Ben. "Thank you for coming over to help so I don't have to."

55

"Yeah. I might have helped if she didn't insist it had to be done with a brush," Matt said. "Rollers look like fun."

"Not really," James said. He didn't look up from the cards he was dealing.

"I don't need more help anyway," Eve said. "Ben's mostly just here to keep me from screwing it up."

"Good luck," Matt muttered. He and James bumped elbows at the joke.

Eve decided they'd had enough greeting. She jerked her head for Ben to follow her again.

"Enjoy the game," he said as he walked away. Then he turned to Eve. "Have you played the 2-player version of *7 Wonders*?"

It was nice that he recognized the game on the table. "The variation where you have an imaginary third player? It's not as much fun."

"No," Ben said. "I mean, I agree it's better with more players, but there's a separate game designed for two that I'm guessing based on your answer you have *not* tried."

"Apparently, that's a good guess." She set down the bucket she was still carrying and gestured into the dining room that wasn't a dining room. "This is our project."

Ben also set down what he carried and walked into the room. He stopped near the dangling light fixture – it had candelabra-shaped bulbs but wasn't overly ornate – and pointed to it. "I see what says dining room to you. This seems like it should have a table under it to keep people from walking into it."

"Simon hit his head on that all the time, but I have the advantage of being short." Eve stepped under the light to demonstrate how it just missed her head.

56

"You're not that short," Ben said.

She was five foot three, which she knew was not super short, but it sometimes felt that way when even her younger brothers towered over her. Ben didn't tower. He was taller than Eve and tall enough to hit his head on the light. But there was nothing about his height that suggested he felt it was an advantage. She mostly noticed that when they both stood near the light, they were also near each other.

"I could swap this out for something closer to the ceiling," he said. "That's more my specialty than painting."

"Um…" She stepped backwards to breathe easier and consider the light from a better angle. "I don't know. I'll probably move out when… uh…" She hoped to move out when she got married, but that was a word that made her uncomfortable at the moment. "I don't know how long I'll live here, and my parents or someone else might want to make it a dining room again."

Ben nodded. "I'd be happy to show off my real skills, but I can settle for painting if that's all you want. Are you ready to get started?"

"Well, you're supposed to tell me where to start."

"First, we protect everything that needs to be protected from paint. With no furniture in here, that'll be easy." He pulled a canvas drop cloth from his bag, and she helped him spread it over the carpet.

Eve had spotted some blue tape in the bucket. She picked up the roll she had bought and showed it to Ben. "I got tape. I'm not completely clueless."

"I didn't think you were. In fact, I… uh…" His eyes darted around the room. "We'll need to tape along the ceiling. Do you have a step ladder or should I get mine from the truck?"

"I'll get one." Eve dashed towards the garage. She didn't grab a coat or put down the tape. The nerves she'd sensed as he hastily switched topics had her mind racing. Had he thought she'd pretended to be clueless as an excuse to ask for his help? Had he hoped that? And she hadn't asked for his help. He offered. Hadn't he? Eve couldn't remember the exact conversation.

She opened the closet at the back of the garage and examined her choices. Wedged behind some old bikes was a standard step ladder. There were various shovels and yard tools lining the closet wall. A shorter 3-step ladder was more accessible. She shivered against the cold and cloudy day. Surely Ben could reach the ceiling with that even if she couldn't. Eve shoved the roll of tape on her arm like a bangle bracelet to free up both hands to grab the ladder.

Ben had already taped about half the baseboard, and he'd removed the curtains. The room felt larger with the extra light. She set the ladder in a corner and started taping around the window. Or rather, she tried to tape around the window. It seemed to be going all over the place. "How do you get this straight?" she asked.

He sat back on his heels to face her. "If you get both ends where you want them, the rest should fall into place."

Eve wadded up the length that had lost some stickiness from all her repositioning. She tore off a new piece to try again. It seemed that one end moved on its own every time she glanced at the other one. She let out a soft groan of frustration. But then she had a vision of Ben putting his hands on hers to guide them. The thought had come out of nowhere. She wasn't trying to think about anything other than the tape. "I'm going to get it," she said, even though Ben certainly hadn't had any ideas of helping.

He got on the ladder and had the bottom and top of the room taped before Eve finished the one window.

The tape she put on did look good, nice and straight. But she wasn't getting faster. Her hands were not steady enough. Once Ben was watching her – still on the other side of the room but doing nothing but watching her – those hands got a little slippery, too.

"I can… I mean, if it's frustrating you… I can take over the tape." He sounded hesitant, wanting to help but only if she wanted help.

Eve *was* frustrated. She did not like looking incompetent. Part of her wanted to keep practicing so she'd get better. But the part of her that had no idea when she'd need this skill again decided it wasn't worth it. "Yes, please." She got up and handed him her tape, even though he was still holding the roll he'd used.

"Should I open the paint?" she asked. She had a screwdriver and was confident she could pry the lid off without embarrassing herself. Unless maybe there was a special paint-opener she didn't have.

"We'll need the plaster first," he said. "It's the white bucket inside the big bucket."

Locating the plaster was simple enough. She also found a metal tool with a black handle that she knew she'd seen someone use to apply plaster at some point, possibly in a movie. She was able to remove the plastic lid with only her fingers.

Ben tossed his tape into the bucket and hers next to it. She tried not to think about how slow she'd be with the plaster. Maybe she should just let him do it all.

"I'll just show you the first one," Ben said. He got some plaster on the corner of the tool, and she followed him to the wall. "Just squish a bit of plaster into the nail hole, then firmly scrape off the excess so it's smooth. Here you go." He handed her the tool with surprising confidence.

Eve found another hole and tried to copy what he'd shown her. It worked! "That looks good, right?"

"Perfect." He nodded approvingly and gestured to the rest of the room. "Only about twenty more to go."

She filled the other holes in no time. She didn't actually pay attention to how long it took, but it seemed fast because she was having fun. She even smoothed out a few dents that maybe didn't need to be smoothed. She was carefully scanning the walls for anything she'd missed when she noticed Ben was laughing.

"What's so funny?"

"You're like almost giddy over that plaster."

She glanced at the window, and then the tape. "It's fun to find something I can actually do."

"Well, I think you've covered everything you can at this point. Ready to paint?"

"Yes." She knew that would be fun, too. And she was pleased to see that he hadn't even opened the can while she went nuts with the plaster. He wasn't rushing her.

He capped the plaster while she pried the lid off the paint. Cheerful Yellow was fairly pale yet still bright. At least that's how Eve would describe it. "What do you think of this color?" she asked Ben. "It's not too girly, is it?"

He looked down at the open can, then wrinkled his eyes as though he didn't understand the question. "It's yellow," he said.

"Yeah, I described it to Drew, and he only replied that it was sufficiently girly. I wasn't sure about the tone of the text, if he meant it was kind of girly or that he was just happy I hadn't gone with hot pink or something. I tried to get him to clarify, and then he just said it was fine." She frowned at the unsatisfying answers.

Ben seemed to give it some thought. "I don't know what he meant either," he said eventually. "Yellow seems pretty... uh... bland to me. But not in a bad way."

"Boring?" She raised her eyebrows threateningly.

"I didn't say that. I think it's great. I meant... I'm used to painting houses we plan to sell, and my dad always picks some shade of off-white to deliberately make it boring so whoever buys the house can do whatever they want with it. I'm kind of excited to paint an actual color. I only meant it was not too bold. No one's going to come in here and be like why did you pick this color because it's too...anything."

Eve smiled at his hasty explanation and appreciated that it made more sense than "sufficiently girly" anyway. She picked up a brush. "Where should I start?"

"A lot of people like to paint around the edges first because that's harder, or at least slower. Then fill in the middle. But you can start wherever you like."

Eve wanted to see her color spread out quickly. She set the can near a wall with no window or doorway and – with a bit more guidance from Ben – had a large patch of Cheerful Yellow in front of her. Ben opened a window while she worked and placed a fan on the sill facing out. The noise and the chill breeze made her work faster.

Ben had transferred paint to a smaller can so he could hold it on the ladder to paint the section Eve couldn't reach from the ground.

"I love that color." Tori stood in the doorway buttoning her coat.

"Thanks," Eve said. "You leaving?"

"Yeah."

"Who won?" Ben asked.

"James, even after all the whining about being stuck with Babylon."

"It wasn't whining." His voice called from another room. "I was simply pointing out that Babylon is the worst."

The three of them shared a smile at his whining protest against whining, which he certainly did on purpose. Then Tori said farewell and Ben and Eve returned to their painting.

6

*E*ve stood near the heating vent that was trying to counter
the open window. She was working hard enough that she
wasn't really cold, but the warm air still felt nice on her legs since
her arms were moving more. She painted slowly to stay in that
spot. Ben moved the ladder and came to refill his paint before he
climbed it again. He used his brush to keep paint from dripping
down the side. Though the canvas on the floor was worn and
dotted with drips and splashes of paint, Eve didn't see any that
matched the yellow they were using.

"I told you how I sometimes watch stupid movies with my
parents, right?" she asked.

"You said some of them aren't stupid."

Her arm moved slower as she talked, and Ben also kept a
slower pace as he listened.

"Yeah, now and then we luck into a good one. And some of
them are so bad they're good. But then there are the ones that are
just bad. All these paint splatters," she waved her hand at the drop
cloth, "remind me of one – well two – of the just bad kind. There
was this scene where two people were flirting by throwing paint at
each other. We agreed it wasn't funny but didn't really… until we

saw a second movie a little later with a similar scene. My dad actually looked it up to see if it had the same writer, and it didn't. So then we were kind of amazed multiple people thought it was somehow charming for adults to act oblivious to a huge mess, some of which couldn't be cleaned up. I mean, this is paint we're talking about, right? It's not like water balloons or something. Of course neither movie showed the cleanup. Now that I'm looking at it in real life, it's even worse. I can imagine exactly how angry I'd be if you suddenly threw that can of paint at me."

Ben nodded, then he pretended to look guilty and said, "It's a good thing you warned me not to."

Eve laughed. But then she realized that they weren't just talking about throwing paint. She'd brought up characters who were flirting. What if Ben's joke was intended that way? She turned and slapped her brush against the wall. "Look at me standing around when there's still a lot of work to do."

She assumed Ben also returned to work. She heard his feet on the ladder but didn't look that direction. The silence was awkward. They'd been working comfortably next to each other until Eve shut down her own topic in a rush. She searched her brain for a new topic, something that had nothing to do with flirting.

"I want to ask you a question," she said, "but it's going to take me a minute to get to the question." Eve glanced up to make sure she had his attention.

He seemed curious and nodded quickly to confirm he was listening.

"Grandpa Will was here for lunch, and he told us this story about how there used to be parking meters by the grocery store, and a penny would get you twelve minutes."

"*Twelve* minutes?"

Eve shrugged. "That's what he said. I have no idea why it wasn't ten or fifteen."

Ben motioned for her to continue with an expression that apologized for interrupting but still didn't understand the random number.

"He said that he'd send one of his kids to watch if the time expired with instructions to only put in another penny if they might get caught. Now please don't think I'm trying to be judgy about what my grandpa did a long time ago. I'm just using the story as, like, a metaphor or something because it got me thinking about a bunch of other stuff. When he told it, my first thought was that he shouldn't be trying to get away with something. But then I was like, it's a penny."

Ben smiled at the tone she used to dismiss the penny.

Eve only lost her train of thought for a moment. "So that got me thinking about sins in general and how we, or at least I, tend to dismiss the little ones as, well, not that bad because it's only a penny. But maybe it's actually worse in some ways because that's kind of like saying God isn't worth the penny, or you know, the penny amount of effort it would take me to avoid that sin. And does that make us more likely to start thinking maybe a nickel isn't so bad either?"

"Well…" Ben paused halfway down the ladder to focus on his answer, once he was sure she was waiting for one. "If I'm following your metaphor correctly, then I think I agree with you. It's like sin inflation. When you convince yourself something isn't *that bad*, you're actually convincing yourself it's not really wrong. Like if…" His mouth kept silently opening as he stopped himself from saying several things before he finally said, "It's probably safer if I stick to the metaphor and not try to use an example. Once you've convinced yourself the penny isn't wrong, the baseline moves and the nickel is like the penny. Will you eventually convince yourself the nickel isn't wrong?"

"Exactly. For a specific example, I..." Eve noticed that she'd stopped painting again to listen. She dipped her brush and tried to keep her hand moving with her mouth. "I got a little addicted to gossip when I was in high school. I hung out with this girl who seemed to be really good at knowing who was dating who and whose parents were splitting up and... I actually convinced myself it was important to be up-to-date on, you know, stuff that wasn't any of my business. I figured it didn't hurt anyone for me to know. But then I was also sharing the things I heard even though I didn't know which things were true. I told myself it was okay as long as I always included a comment about how it might just be a rumor. And then I got caught, um..." Her face flushed at the embarrassing memory. "I'd started eavesdropping to get more information to share because I was actually jealous that my friend knew things before me, and someone confronted me, and... well, it was humiliating but caused me to take a closer look at what my conscience had been telling me all along."

"Sounds like a hard way to learn a lesson," Ben said. His voice was kind. There didn't seem to be censure for her past behavior but possible admiration that she'd admitted it.

Eve wanted to be completely honest. "I still... well, I try to ask myself a lot whether or not information directly affects me or the person I'm talking to. And I... I can't stop myself from trying to get Noah to admit he's finally dating Sarah Franks. It's not exactly my business, but he is my cousin and I work with him

66

and… I don't want to tell everyone. I just want to be happy for him."

"I'm sure he'll tell you when he's ready."

"I know he'll have to invite me to a wedding, but I'd rather not wait that long." Eve did understand the desire for privacy. The more people you told when you started dating someone, the more people you might need to tell if you got dumped. And sometimes pressure to convince people it was going well could cause problems. It probably wouldn't bother her so much if she didn't suspect that Noah wasn't keeping quiet for privacy but only because he knew it bothered her that he wouldn't tell her.

"Oh, my goodness, you guys aren't even halfway done."

Eve turned to Matt, who was standing in the doorway surveying the progress. "There was a lot of prep work," she said. "We might be halfway done even if we're not halfway done painting."

Her brother raised his eyebrows skeptically. He said, "I thought you were making it pink."

"I never said that."

"Mom said you needed a, uh… what'd she call it? A feminine sanctuary?"

"I don't," Eve said. "And if I did, it wouldn't have to be pink."

"Isn't that your favorite color?"

"My favorite color is purple."

Matt put on a deadly serious expression. "I hate to be the one to tell you this, but that's not purple."

Ben laughed behind her.

"Just because it's my favorite color doesn't mean I need everything to be purple."

"I'm not sure you need an extra room now either," Matt said. "You're barely outnumbered now that Simon moved out."

"I still have too many brothers even if they don't all live with me," Eve said. She was kidding. She loved her brothers, and even the youngest one knew it.

He laughed. "Hey, speaking of brothers, are Drew and Aiden coming home for Thanksgiving?"

"No. Finals are only a week later. They don't want to make the drive twice so close."

Matt nodded understandingly. "I guess I'll let you get back to work." He put air quotes on the last word.

Eve realized she was standing around again. She'd even let her brush drip on the floor, which she was very glad was covered. She rolled her eyes at herself as she slapped her brush on the wall a bit harder than necessary. "I don't know what's wrong with me today," she said. "I assure you I'm perfectly capable of making pizza and talking at the same time."

"You do have more practice at that," Ben said.

Moving a brush up and down shouldn't take that much concentration, but she supposed Ben had a point. This was new, a new experience. Ben had painted many rooms. "I guess practice explains why you don't seem to be stopping as often."

"That and I have to keep working. I only got invited over to help. Don't want to get kicked out for slacking." He flashed a grin.

Eve smiled at the joke. But she was happy they'd just established an excuse for her eyes to stay focused on her work. There had been something searching in his tone, something that tried to ask if there could be any other reason he was there. The unspoken question made Eve's stomach flip and her conscience squeeze. She only had to walk this line a few more weeks.

"I love this color!" Eve's mom was now checking the progress.

"Thanks," Eve said.

"When you showed me the sample, I was afraid it was going to be a bright yellow room that was maybe a bit overwhelming, but this is… nice. It's not bright yellow, it's just… bright."

Ben peeked at Eve to see how she was enjoying the praise. She soaked it up, but she didn't get a chance to thank her mom again before she walked fully into the room and set a hand on the ladder Ben was on.

"You, young man, are doing an excellent job here, which is really why I came in. I heard someone mention Thanksgiving. It reminded me that we could use a few strong guys to carry the boxes out to the truck tomorrow night. We had plenty of volunteers to sort and fill the boxes, but most of them…"

"You can get Matt and James to help if you need more guys to carry the full ones," Eve interrupted. "They like to show off their muscles." Eve had let her mom talk for a bit because she'd enjoyed the deer-in-the-headlights expression on Ben's face when she approached. But she had promised to run interference and would keep her word.

"I already told them they were going to help, but we can never have too much help." Eve's mom kept her eyes on Ben.

"Ben is here to help me paint, not for anything else."

"This project will be done today, and I'm looking for help tomorrow. You're not busy, are you?" She continued to look only at Ben. "We have short shifts so you can come from four to six or six to eight."

Ben didn't open his mouth. He looked concerned that either answer would be wrong. His eyes flicked to Eve.

69

"Mom!" Eve didn't let him worry for more than a second. "Not now. It's not fair to corner him when he's already helping me."

Her mom backed up several steps and released her stare. "Fine. I'll let you two paint." She winked at Eve as she turned to leave. It appeared she'd been more interested in scaring Ben than actually getting him to volunteer.

Ben came down the ladder to reposition it. He lowered his voice before he climbed it again. "I didn't agree to something by not saying anything, did I?"

"No. I think she was just messing with you anyway."

"She was…" His eyes tracked where Eve's mom had been and where she disappeared. Then he shook his head at his lack of response. He painted in silence for a minute before he said, "I feel I need to clarify that I do help out at the church sometimes. I set up Bingo tables with Sebastian a few times, and I'm a regular reader. It's just… I don't like to agree to stuff when I don't have any time to think about it."

Eve smiled at the defense – and a little at memories of him reading at Mass – and said, "I know. Just because you don't want to have your arm twisted doesn't make you lazy."

"Eve!" James' voice called out a moment before he arrived in the room to continue the stream of family members. "I can't find the green basketball. Next time you talk to Drew, ask him if he has it."

"Why don't you just ask him?"

"You're the one who likes to gab," he said. "Now you actually have a reason to call him."

"First of all, I don't need a reason to call my brother. Second of all, that's a pretty lame reason." Eve was standing in the draft of the open window and as she talked to James, she saw past him that a light snowfall had started. "Are you going to the park in the snow?"

He shook his head. "There's an open gym after school tomorrow. I wanted to put a ball by my bag so I don't forget in the morning." He gave an affected sigh. "I guess I'll have to take a normal one."

She was amused by his fake dejection. Her eyes stayed on the window after he left, watching the big scattered flakes. It was somewhat mesmerizing, watching the flakes crash into the grass in total silence. But it also made her cold. Perhaps it wasn't the best time of year for a project that required ventilation. Perhaps she shouldn't have spent the last two months only thinking about what to do with the room. She shivered, and she had a thought of Ben putting his arm around her shoulder to warm her up.

Eve pushed the thought away and turned around to focus on acceptable thoughts of painting a room. But she found that Ben was looking at her. She was flooded with the ridiculous fear that he'd somehow seen the previous thought through the back of her head.

"Why is it green?" he asked.

"Why is it green?" She didn't know why she thought repeating the question would help her follow it.

"The basketball," Ben prompted. "Is that a team color?"

"No. It's a punishment color."

He laughed at what he didn't understand because he sensed a good story.

"It was several years ago now," Eve said. "The older boys lost two balls in one summer. They took them to the park and let someone else take them home I guess." She shrugged. "I wasn't there so I don't know exactly how it happened. They just lost track of who they belonged to or something. The second time it happened, my dad was kind of annoyed. He replaced the ball with a green one. He told the boys there was far less chance anyone would mistake it for theirs. I guess Simon was kind of embarrassed about it and ended up buying himself a regular orange one. Matt and James seem to think it's cool to have a more unique ball." She'd gotten her brush into the paint and on the wall while she finished the story, and Eve took a moment to be proud of herself for the work. Then she took another moment to scoff that being able to paint and talk at the same time could be a source of pride.

They talked strategy for a minute, who was going to paint where, as they moved onto the last wall. Ben had painted all the edges, leaving the easier and more fun parts for Eve. As they tackled the last section together, no one suggested it was a race, but Eve felt her hand moving faster to prove she'd do her share.

"Nice!" Eve's dad was the last to comment on the progress.

She flashed him a smile at his approval without fully turning around so she could keep painting.

"Looks like you might finish up just in time for dinner," he said. He flipped on the light as he spoke.

Eve hadn't noticed how dark it had gotten. Apparently, it *was* approaching dinnertime.

"You should stay and join us, Ben. Susanna is making burgers so I'll need to know how many you want."

Ben stopped working at the invitation. He sent Eve a questioning look, probably because he knew her mom's name was not Susanna.

"He calls the grill Susanna," she explained. "He likes to talk about it like it's a person."

72

"And she gets offended when Eve talks about her like she's not a person." He shook his head with disappointment.

Eve laughed. "Are you sure you want to grill when it's snowing?"

"It stopped," he said.

That was true. Eve saw no more flakes falling. The ground dusted with white still didn't seem like an ideal grilling environment to her, but her dad had ventured out in thunderstorms when the mood struck.

"So... Ben? Is one burger enough for you?"

Ben nodded slowly. "Uh... yeah. That sounds good. Thanks."

"What about you, Eve? You haven't worked up a bigger than usual appetite in here?"

"No. One's good for me," she said. She tossed a thank you over her shoulder as well, still determined to keep the yellow moving towards Ben.

His movements seemed to slow as he leaned towards Eve with a quiet voice. "Has he taken lessons from your mom or are they both naturally good at, uh... not waiting for answers?"

Eve considered what had just happened. Ben was staying for dinner without having actually agreed. He could have easily said no thank you to the number of burgers though. Surely he hadn't felt trapped. But that got her thinking of whether or not or how much he might want to be there, of how much he might want to spend the extra time with Eve. And then she worried what topics would come up during dinner. What was her dad thinking when he invited Ben to stay? She dodged the questions she was taking too long to answer anyway. "You don't have other plans, do you?"

"No." He surveyed the progress, something like disappointment in his expression. "I should probably let my parents know not to wait on me though." He set his brush on the paint can and checked his hands for paint before he pulled a phone from his pocket.

There was only a small patch of unpainted wall. Eve tried to finish before he could text his parents. Turning that final square yellow matched the satisfaction of putting in the last piece of a jigsaw puzzle. She was nearly there when Ben's brush collided with hers. They painted with the brushes pushing against each other in a friendly competition to get that last bit of white. Eve laughed as she backed up into a freshly painted room.

"I think we're done," Ben said.

"With the painting anyway." She held her brush uncertainly. "What's the best way to start the cleanup? And can I take the tape off right away?"

Ben nodded, possibly at her second question. He glanced around and appeared to be assessing the situation. "Why don't you go ahead and peel off all the tape while I wash out the brushes?" He took the brush to free up her hands. "Make sure you're aware of any wet paint on the tape so you don't smear it on the woodwork or touch something after it gets on your fingers."

"Right," Eve said. "I probably would have figured that out, but I might have figured it out the hard way." She smiled her appreciation, then decided to start where the paint should be most dry and work her way around the room, treating it all as though it was wet. It didn't take long for her to get paint on her fingers. She was careful to touch nothing but tape – and maybe the ladder that already had paint splotches from earlier use – as she gathered it all into a big ball.

74

Ben put the lid on the paint and folded the drop cloth into a pile in the center of the room. He'd also ripped the tape off where the wall met the ceiling when he realized, before Eve did, that she wouldn't be able to reach that strip. He put on his coat before he took the brushes outside. Eve didn't register that he meant to use the outdoor spigot or how cold that would be until a few minutes later. She was thinking about how quickly Ben worked when he was focused and how he hadn't complained even once about her slow pace. She threw out all the tape and washed her hands. Then she stood in the dining room that might not be a dining room to admire the new paint. It looked great. It also looked empty, but that was a problem for another day.

Her mom had already set the table for dinner so Eve went to the back window to check on her dad's progress with the grill. Ben was standing next to him, holding his red hands over the flames to warm them. Eve folded her arms across her chest. She felt a shiver just thinking about having wet hands in winter weather. She probably would have used the kitchen sink, which probably would have made her mom frown. Had Ben taken the brushes outside to spare her mom the grief or had he thought of Eve when he did it? *Or* did he regularly wash things outside in his work and only thought it was normal?

"He's a nice guy." Eve felt her mom's arm wrap around her shoulders as she spoke from behind.

"Yeah." Eve kept watching out the window to avoid any insinuation that might be on her mom's face. Ben was laughing at something her dad said.

"He seems to like you."

"I think we've talked enough he considers me a friend," Eve said. She knew that wasn't what her mom meant, but she wasn't going to go there.

"And you? Do you consider him a *friend*?" It seemed her mom was going there.

Eve sighed. She still didn't turn away from the window. "Of course, Mom. We can be friends."

"I don't think you can blame me for being concerned that someone's going to get hurt."

"I'm not going to hurt Ben." Eve wouldn't hurt him intentionally. But she couldn't even ask him how he felt, which made it hard to protect whatever feelings might exist. The conversation needed to end because he was holding a plate for her dad to stack finished burgers. They were about to come inside.

The arm slipped off Eve's shoulders as her mom moved to call the boys to dinner. First she said, "I wasn't talking about Ben."

$\mathcal{N}$oah was early as usual. He walked up to Dan before he'd even taken off his coat. "We'll wrap them."

"No," Dan said. "Wrap what?"

"You're going to say no before you even know what I'm talking about?"

"You're too excited for this to be a good idea." Dan put his eyes back on the screen where he was ordering supplies. "This is something you thought of on the way here and haven't yet thought *through*."

"We can wrap the Christmas pizzas." Noah did sound excited. "In wrapping paper, like presents."

Dan sighed loudly. "That would be a hassle. And the steam from the pizzas would make the paper soggy. No one wants to unwrap a soggy present."

"Maybe foil paper? I'm going to think about this more." Noah didn't sound ready to give up. He unzipped his coat as he walked towards the back with a determined expression.

Eve smiled to herself. The exchange she'd just witnessed would make great fodder for her next post. Wrapping the pizzas was a terrible idea. Rather than making fun of Noah for it, she'd focus on making Dan look good, maybe he saved customers from the bad idea, like Superman. No. Mighty Mouse. She'd put Dan's head on Mighty Mouse flying away with a pizza box. Noah would be on the ground with a roll of wrapping paper. She was considering a few different speech bubbles to add when Noah started slicing peppers near her.

"By the way, you're welcome," she said.

He snorted. "What are you implying I need to thank you for?"

"You can thank me by admitting you're dating Sarah."

Noah continued chopping in silence.

"Fine. You're thanking me for not pointing out to your dad that to properly wrap a present, you need to put the seam on the bottom, which involves turning the box upside-down. You know what happens when you turn a pizza box upside-down, right?"

The knife stopped moving for a moment as he seemed to internally acknowledge the flaw in his plan. He started cutting again as he said, "I've already moved on from wrapping them. I think we can stick a bow to the top – and don't say the bag would crush it, I've already worked that into the plan – but I'll give Dad time to recover before I explain how I've improved the idea."

Eve liked the bow idea, or maybe some pretty ribbon around the box. She didn't tell Noah that because she didn't want him to mention her approval when he next brought it up with Dan. Their debates were far more entertaining when no one tried to drag her in. Her next cartoon could have Noah yelling after the Mighty Mouse Dan something about how he could fix it.

Her shift only overlapped an hour with Noah's. He hadn't said anything to Dan about a bow before she left. She had the exact image she wanted to post in her head by the time she got home. The house was empty as the rest of her family was loading Thanksgiving boxes at the church.

Eve was on her own for dinner. She grabbed an apple and made a peanut butter sandwich. She sat on the floor in her newly yellow room while she ate. It didn't take her long, but she enjoyed the silence that surrounded her. Memories of the previous day flooded the silence until she began to fear she was enjoying it too much.

She put her plate in the dishwasher and created her new post. Rather than holding a roll of wrapping paper, she managed to get a recognizable Noah wrapped up in the paper with eyes that matched the candy cane pattern. It looked as though he'd been possessed by the paper, sort of a candy cane villain that had required the intervention of Mighty Mouse Dan. It made her laugh. Hopefully, that was a sign others would also be amused. She responded coyly to a question about the first day the Christmas pizza would be available.

Then she checked the text from Ben she'd been pretending not to have noticed. He said he'd decided to go to the later shift at the church in case his help was needed and asked if he'd see her there. That shift had already started. Eve was tempted to get her coat and rush to the church. She knew that was a bad idea. It would be obvious that she'd only decided to help after seeing that Ben would be there. She simply replied that she knew him being there would make her mom happy and thanked him for that.

It might have been because she felt guilty about wanting to talk to Ben that she decided to try to talk to someone else. Aiden didn't answer his phone, probably because it wasn't Wednesday. He did have one evening class, but Eve couldn't remember for sure if that was on Mondays. She settled for talking to his voicemail.

"James wanted me to ask Drew if he has the green basketball. I know he won't answer, and I thought you might have seen it if he does have it. Don't worry about calling me back because it's not that important. Just something I thought of. I'll just talk to you on Wednesday. Have a good night."

She hung up and called Drew. Of course he didn't answer. She left him a message asking about the green basketball, too. Then she set her phone next to her and stared at the yellow wall across from her. She wasn't really looking at it. Her mind was ignoring her eyes in favor of her conscience. Was waiting still the right thing to do? Was it actually a lie of omission if she didn't tell Ben? It felt like clear betrayal if she *did* tell him. She didn't have much longer to wait now. And yet that thought made her feel bad, too.

She picked up her phone again and texted Sarah to point out another review the flowers and pizza combo had received. Then she texted Grandpa Will to ask what he thought of her new cartoon. She also asked Tori if she was coming for Thanksgiving even though she was 99% sure she was.

When she couldn't think of anyone else to contact, she checked her post and saw it already had three comments. One person demanded to know what the heck was going on at Pans and Plates. She demanded with several laughing faces so Eve took that as appreciation. One person asked why Dan was dressed as Superman and Micky Mouse at the same time. The third person incorrectly interpreted the picture to mean Noah wanted to make a pizza covered with crushed candy canes.

Eve smiled at the reactions. She'd wait a day to see which direction the conversation went before she added to it. She put the phone down and stared at the wall again without looking at it again. Her mind jumped from something she didn't want to think about to something she shouldn't want to think about and back and forth until she decided to get her mind onto something else entirely.

She got up to figure out where she'd left her bible. It was in the kitchen. She brought it back to the floor of her empty room and opened to the bookmark. The bookmark was a list of books that she crossed off as she finished them since she wasn't reading in order. Two chapters of Chronicles didn't provide any particular spiritual insight. But she did find calm. She set the bible aside in favor of her blank notebook in case she felt compelled to start sketching out a plan for the room in front of her.

Pans and Plates was closed Thursday and Friday. She'd help her mom as much as she could with the Thanksgiving meal, but maybe Friday would be a good time to take the next step on making the room usable. If she could figure out what the next step should be. What did she want in this pretty yellow room? At the moment, she wanted a more comfortable place to sit.

That wasn't an entirely new or novel thought. Eve had considered before that anything she put in this room could be something she took with her when she eventually moved out. She'd need a couch or some comfortable chairs when she didn't have her parents' furniture. But buying furniture sounded expensive and grown-up and a little scary. Maybe she would plan to just browse in one or two stores. Maybe she'd test the waters, get some ideas. Maybe she'd find something she loved that would make it less scary.

The back door banged open and heavy footsteps stomped through the kitchen. Her brothers' laughing voices announced their arrival on top of the other noises. Eve assumed her parents were with them and their presence was drowned out by the boys' conversation.

Matt appeared in the doorway by Eve. "I can see why you were too busy to help at the church," he joked.

"I'm brainstorming," she said. "It's very hard work."

"That explains the burnt rubber smell," James said as he stepped into the doorway, too. "Trying to use something that hasn't been used in a long time doesn't go well."

Eve smiled at their teasing. She helped enough that they couldn't make her feel guilty for not helping this time.

"Enjoy your sunshine paint fumes," Matt said as they both walked away.

The room did in fact smell strongly of fresh paint. Eve had been in there so long she barely noticed it. She was going to get up when she saw a new text from Grandpa Will, three actually. Two were the picture she sent him sent back with no reply. The third said, "What harpooned the boyy wiith VVHIstmsss pizza mow?" It contained his usual extra spaces between words. The last word must have had twenty spaces before it.

Eve sighed as she tried to parse what he was telling her. Grandpa Will had a magnifying glass he used to read the texts he received, but he couldn't seem to bother to use it on the ones he sent. She felt like she was nagging if she asked for clarification, or why he didn't want to see what he was sending.

This one seemed easier than some once she put in the effort. The boy was probably referring to Noah. Did Grandpa Will think her post implied something happened to Noah rather than him happening to the pizza?

Ben called while she was pondering a reply. Eve answered quickly. "Hi, Ben. Can you help me figure out what Grandpa Will is trying to ask?"

She heard him chuckle. "What words *can* you read?"

"It's better than some," Eve said. "I asked his opinion on my latest post and he sent me pictures of it so I think it's safe to conclude his reply is related. It starts with 'what harpooned the boy,' which I assume means what happened to the boy, Noah, and it ends with mow, which I think meant now. He seems to be asking what happened to Noah now. Except... there's some extra gibberish between boy and now with random capital letters on one word that... wait a minute... I bet he's capitalizing Christmas for Christmas pizza. Oh! He wants to know what happened to Noah's Christmas pizza now. I guess I just needed to talk it out."

"I called just in time then," Ben said. "Glad I could help."

Eve laughed at his playfully smug tone.

"What *did* happen to the Christmas pizza," Ben asked. "Your meme looked like Dan took it away. Is he not going to do it after all?"

"Hmm. Maybe it's not as funny as I thought if no one gets it. Noah wanted to wrap the pizzas up like presents, and Dan saved them from that disaster. Can you imagine peeling soggy paper off your pizza? Very appetizing."

"Well, it'd only be on the box, but... yeah... I don't think I want anything that makes the pizza harder to get to." Ben seemed to give it more thought than Noah had before he brought it up. "It's funnier now that I get it. Maybe you needed some paper trailing off the pizza as he flew away to show where Noah was trying to put it."

"Maybe." Eve tried to picture that.

"But I still laughed when I first saw it, especially Dan's head on Mighty Mouse, who I totally had to look up. How do you know about a flying mouse from the 40s anyway?"

"Drew was into vintage cartoons for a while."

83

"How did your mom talk everyone else into helping tonight and not you?" he asked.

"I was still at work when they left." Eve thought there was some implication that he had missed her. But it didn't necessarily mean anything so she tried not to hear any meaning.

"It looked like the food drive was pretty successful. Are you expecting a lot of family at your house for Thanksgiving?"

"Just local family… which is still a lot. Grandpa Will, Simon and Tori, John and Anna and their kids, plus Noah's whole family. Mom will get out the fancy plates, and we'll have a lot of leftovers."

"Sounds good."

"Yeah. I think you said you're expecting houseguests," Eve said. "When are they coming?"

"Tomorrow. I'll need to move some things into Nate's room in the morning so my parents can take over mine. Mom is afraid that her mom can't handle the stairs so my grandparents are getting their downstairs bedroom."

"That's a lot of shuffling," Eve said.

"It'll only be three nights so it's really not too bad except… uh… Nate and I have already made a bet about how many times Nana will say something to the effect of, 'You shouldn't have gone to so much trouble,' or 'We could have stayed in a hotel.'"

Eve laughed at his high falsetto impression. "Does your grandma really sound like that?"

"Uh… no. She has a southern accent."

She laughed more. "Are you doing anything special with your grandparents, other than the big meal?"

"Not really. We don't have any work planned so we'll have time together. And we'll take them out to see the house that's about ready to flip. I think they'll like that. Though Nana's bound

84

to say something borderline offensive about how surprised she is that Nate and I are capable of, you know, doing anything."

"What do you mean?"

"Well, last time they were here, we showed them a house that wasn't as far along. I pointed out a light fixture still in a box and showed her where I was going to put it. She was all, 'Gasp, you can do that all by yourself?'"

Eve laughed as he went back to the high-pitched impression.

"I had to remind her I'm a trained electrician who went to school and everything," he said. "It shouldn't surprise anyone that I have some basic skills in that area. Then she said something about how *cute* Nate's tool belt was, like it was something he had for show."

Ben would be cute wearing a tool belt, but Eve didn't mean it the way his grandmother did. The thought made her face warm. She banished it and tried to focus on the grandmother. "I've had some relatives act like I'm still a kid, too," she said.

"We are the youngest of her grandkids," Ben conceded, "and we're not really offended by anything she says. We just laugh."

"Sometimes when I find myself getting annoyed with Grandpa Will's incoherent texts, I remind myself that he might not be around to annoy me much longer."

"Yeah." He exhaled slowly. "That's a way to be more appreciative, but it's not a pleasant thought for sure."

"Here's something pleasanter. Uh… more pleasant. I made a decision about my room."

"Your not a dining room?"

"Uh-huh. I'm going to use my day off on Friday to go to at least one furniture store where I will try to get inspiration on what kind of seating I might want in here." She ran her hand over the wall that somehow seemed smoother with the new paint.

Ben made some snorting noises that sounded as though he was trying not to laugh, and not trying very hard.

"What's so funny?" Eve asked.

"I'm waiting for the decision part. You're saying you want to look at some things and think about some things. That doesn't sound very decisive."

"I *decided*... to look at things." Eve was a little defensive, though she made herself sound more so to continue his amusement. "I've been just looking at the empty room for months. Now it's yellow, *and* I'm going to look at furniture. That feels like progress to me."

He admitted that looking at real furniture was closer to progress than the nothing she'd been doing. He stressed the nothing to tease her more. But then he told her about a place he knew with a large showroom and suggested she bring a tape measure so if she saw something she liked she'd know how it would fit. That reminded him of a house they'd bought a few years earlier with a broken couch.

The upholstery had been peeled off part of the back and one of the support boards sawed in two. Ben's dad had speculated that someone tried to cut it in half to make it easier to move, then gave up when they realized it'd be impossible to put back together. His mom had guessed that someone lost something inside the couch years ago and when they decided not to take it with them, they used the opportunity to retrieve the lost item. Regardless of what had happened, Ben and Nate had shredded what remained of the couch just for fun.

Eve enjoyed a few other stories. It usually sounded as though Ben liked the tearing apart phase better than the putting things back together phase of remodeling houses. And he preferred finding electrical problems to fix more than simply checking off perfect wiring.

The lighting changed as something switched off in the hallway. Eve wondered at her parents going to bed so early before she checked the time and saw that it wasn't early. She'd been talking to Ben for well over an hour.

"Oh, gosh," she said. "It's later than I thought. I have to work tomorrow so I need to say goodnight."

"But you're not working Friday, right? I'll see you at St. Jude's after the shopping?"

"Yep. See you then." The young adult group had taken a poll to see who would be available the Friday after Thanksgiving and decided they'd still have enough to meet. Though they intended to end early to walk over to the annual town lighting.

Eve saw that Drew and Aiden had both texted that they thought Simon had the green basketball. She put her phone away and went to bed without worrying about progress on that front.

*D*an did one of those slow blinks that meant his eyes were sighing. "A bowl?"

"No, a *bow*." Noah waved his fingers in the air in what appeared to be an attempt to draw a bow.

"Okay." Dan sounded relieved. "I thought you wanted to talk me into turning the Christmas pizza inside out, and we're still not doing that. What do you want to do with a bow?"

"I love how the broccoli-speckled crust came out," Noah said. "It's a great touch of green with the red and green toppings. But it's still not quite as festive as I'd hoped."

"Uh… how is it you're surprised that broccoli doesn't scream festive?" Dan said dryly.

Eve had to catch herself from laughing out loud. She needed to remember that line. On the first day the Christmas pizzas were available, she would post a stalk of broccoli in a Santa hat screaming "Festive!" probably at another picture of Dan's head on the Grinch's body. He'd laughed at how many people had helpfully provided that image for her last time.

"I know you didn't like the wrapping paper," Noah said. "I

think it'd be better to just stick a bow on top of each box. Red or green bows."

Thoughts were clearly chasing through Dan's head as he considered the idea. Noah pulled a pizza out of the oven and began to slice it while he waited. Eve hoped Dan would think long enough for her to concentrate on the four different sections of toppings she was creating.

Finally, he said, "I think we could slap bows on them pretty easily for people who pick them up. But they'd get crushed by the delivery bag."

"Not if we put the bow on right at the door." Noah smiled triumphantly to have an answer ready for this objection. "The driver can *wear* the bows – I'm thinking on a string around the neck or stuck to a hat – and then pull one off to stick to the box right as it comes out of the bag. Instant festive pizza and the driver is festive, too, with the extra bows for the sake of anyone who ordered a boring, non-festive pizza."

"Now you need to stop saying the word festive."

Eve planned that her next post would be a simple announcement that festive had been added to the list of words people were not allowed to say in front of Dan. Jolly and merry were already on the list.

"It's getting hard to talk about Christmas here," Noah said.

Dan frowned at him for a moment, then turned around to greet a customer.

"He's thinking about it," Noah said to Eve. "The bows are gonna happen."

"Maybe," she said, "and maybe I won't quote you on that."

He snorted. "You'll only quote me if it doesn't happen."

She smiled sweetly. She was glad both he and Dan continued to be good sports about everything she posted. She hoped she'd never take a joke too far.

The quartered pizza Eve made was for a man named John Smith. He was a regular customer so she knew John was actually his middle name. After seeing a more interesting first name on his credit card a few times, she'd asked why he preferred something that sounded like a fake name. He said his dad had the same name, and he liked being asked if he was in the witness protection program better than being called Junior.

When he came in to pick up the pizza, he greeted Eve, then called out to Dan in the back. "Hi! You having a jolly day?"

Dan walked towards the front to chat while Eve boxed up the pizza. "I am because I didn't have to make your train wreck of a pizza. Your kids can't just get cheese like other picky eaters?"

"They could," John said, "but they're more jolly when they each get the toppings they like. And I'm merry when I don't have to buy four pizzas – or even two – to make it happen." He gave Eve an appreciative nod as he tapped his credit card to the reader.

The appreciation might have been as much for the tip about how to bother Dan as for making his kids' dinner. Eve smiled graciously rather than laugh at all three of them trying to pretend they didn't know what he was doing.

"Have a good night," Dan said as he pushed the box towards John.

John picked it up with a wink. "Stay jolly, man."

Dan's smile disappeared as soon as the man's back was turned. He glared at Eve.

"I'm sure I have lots of work to do." She scurried back to start a new order, not because she was actually intimidated but because she owed him the satisfaction of feeling intimidating.

Dan left for the night a bit later. With Noah running in and out on delivery duty, Eve was essentially in charge. The teenage employees she was left with seemed to need even more direction than usual. She remembered talking to Ben about people occasionally treating her like a kid. Nothing made her feel more mature and adult than pointing out that pans needing to be washed shouldn't have to be pointed out before someone started washing them.

Pans and Plates closed at nine on Wednesdays. Eve was able to leave within a few minutes. Her parents were already calling it a night when she got home.

"We need to get up early to put the turkey in the oven," her dad said.

"But you will enjoy yelling at the other half of this movie with us tomorrow night." Eve's mom pointed at the now-dark TV. "I predict we're about to find out the guy was a jerk in high school because his dad had just died so he'll be all sympathetic, and she'll choose him."

"Choose him?" Eve asked. "There's two guys in this one?"

"The one who's nice and the one who's fake nice." Her dad rolled his eyes as he headed up the stairs. "It's hard to root for the woman who can't see through it."

"She will."

"Are Matt and James here?" Eve thought the house was suspiciously quiet.

"They had a sudden desire to go bowling."

"I'll probably stay up just long enough to report on when they get home," Eve said. "Goodnight, Mom."

She smiled as she said goodnight because, fortunately, Matt and James could be trusted to be home on time so everyone knew Eve was kidding. She went to her yellow room to make her weekly phone calls. She called Drew first since she knew that would be quick. She spoke to his voicemail. "Hi, Drew. Simon confirmed that he has the green basketball. He said he needed it because you took his to school. Maybe you guys should write your names on things. Anyway, happy Thanksgiving!"

Aiden did answer. "Hi, Eve. I guess it's Wednesday."

"Simon said he has the green basketball because Drew took his," she said. "Do you know if he's right?"

"The ball we've been using does say Simon on it. That's probably his."

Eve decided not to say anything about that. She was already way too involved in basketballs she didn't care about. "Are you expecting a good feast tomorrow? I forget if that's lunch or dinner."

"It starts at four so I'll skip lunch to have lots of room," Aiden said. "Last year there was more pie than anything else, and we got to take home a whole one that was leftover. I wouldn't mind if that happens again."

"I peeked in the kitchen earlier, and it looks like we have pecan and cherry here. Plus, Grandpa Will said he's making his famous pumpkin to bring."

"Famous because it's on the back of the can, right?"

"Yeah. He tells that same joke every year." Eve smiled at how the repetition made it funnier.

"Have you gotten any interesting texts from him?"

"It did take me a minute to figure out the one about the pumpkin pie. I remember pumpkin started with o. But I could tell

92

he was making something, and he got pie right so it was an easy guess."

"Well, I have an essay that's due tonight."

"The day before Thanksgiving?" Eve said. "You have a mean professor."

He laughed. "Kind of. It'd be worse to be due the day after, I think."

"Yeah. I'll let you get to work on it."

"Goodnight, Eve."

That had been quick, too. Eve suspected she still had time before Matt and James got home, not that she was really waiting up for them. She preferred not to have them walk in laughing loudly before they realized everyone else was in bed at the same time she was drifting off to sleep. Since they were supposed to be back at ten, they'd likely come in about 9:50. Eve tapped Ben's number without thinking about much besides the time she had to kill. It rang a few times, but she didn't get voicemail.

"I hope it's not a bad time for you," she said. "Are you with your grandparents?"

"No. They're playing Euchre with my parents right now. And I'm not sure there's a bad time to hear from you."

"You can be the first to know. I'm about to post that the word festive is now banned from Pans and Plates."

Ben laughed. "I think you're having too much fun listening to people try to make those words sound like a natural part of picking up a pizza."

"Some of them don't try very hard."

"Do you think Dan is banning words on purpose now?"

"That… is not something I've considered." She voiced her thoughts as they came to her. "Dan is really smart, and he's figured

93

out people were bugging him with merry and jolly on purpose. He even said the other day that if people wanted to spend money on his pizza just to tell him how jolly he was, then he'd put up with it. On the other hand, Noah was saying festive a lot, and Dan's reaction to that seemed genuine."

"Maybe *Noah* is trying to get words banned," Ben suggested.

Eve gasped at that possibility. It felt more likely, but she did not like the idea of either of her relatives using her. She wanted to be the one in control of the game. Then again, they all had the same goal of keeping the business running successfully so it shouldn't matter. "I'm going to pretend you didn't say that because I can play along better if I don't feel like I'm being manipulated."

"Uh, yeah, manipulated sounds darker than what I meant."

"Did you show the latest house to your grandparents?" Eve asked. "And did they behave?"

"Yes. On both counts. They both said we did a nice job and didn't sound overly surprised. Nana has mentioned that they could have stayed in a hotel twice already though. Two more times and I'm going to have to help Mom put up the Christmas lights."

"What does... oh..." Eve remembered the bet. "Four was Nate's guess?"

"Yeah. I only guessed three so I don't want her using them up too fast."

"Why is putting up Christmas lights for the loser though? That's fun."

Ben sighed loudly into the phone. "Not with my mom. She likes to do something different every year and doesn't plan it out ahead of time. There's a lot of... Try these lights over there. Climb up that ladder and see if this string will go all the way across the porch. Can't we measure the string to see if it'll fit? It's easier if you just put them up there. It's easier because you're not the one climbing up and down the ladder. But I need to see what they look like to know if I want them there. On second thought, pull that string out of the bushes and put the white lights there."

Eve cracked up at the mimicked banter with his mom. It sounded as though Ben had some great memories buried under the complaints. "I wonder if I'll be able to help with the decorating here. They might do it without me while I'm furniture shopping."

"Count your blessings if they do."

"I'm sure the decorating will take more time than the shopping," Eve said. "I'll get Mom to save the funnest parts for me."

"What do you consider the funnest parts?"

"Hmm." She could tell Ben was genuinely interested so she gave it some thought rather than simply saying she liked all of it. "Wrapping presents might be my favorite," she said, "especially the ones not in boxes."

"Wait. You mean the hard ones?"

"I mean the ones you don't have to wrap the standard way. Like something soft like a t-shirt you can roll up and tie the ends like a Tootsie Roll. And once I took a necklace and folded it up into the body of a paper-airplane-shaped present. Took Tori a minute to figure out there was something inside."

"Did you know that someone invented this thing called a gift bag?" Ben said. "You don't have to wrap odd-shaped things at all."

"Those are for people with no imagination."

Ben laughed at the jab. "Efficiency is good, too. Hey. Are we walking to the town lighting from the church?"

"I think so. Um..." Something in his tone caused Eve to imagine that he was talking about the two of them walking alone.

She needed to clarify that they were talking about the plan for the whole group. "The people with kids might want to drive, but most of us will walk."

"Do you usually go… or would you go to it if the group wasn't?"

"Probably." Eve had been most years. All the lights on Main Street – at least a dozen poles were wrapped with lights and garland draped here and there – turned on at exactly 8 o'clock the Friday after Thanksgiving. There would be several food trucks and a local band leading carols. There would also be someone dressed as Santa in front of the police station. "I've been most years, but I usually don't stay long."

"You only go for the lights?"

"Exactly."

"Um…" He chuckled lightly. "I thought you might give me a hard time about the fact that I haven't been since I was a kid. I'm just not big on crowds. But you *only* go to look at the lights you can see every night for the next six weeks or so?"

"Yeah."

"But you work on Main Street," he said. "Those lights will be right out your window."

"There's a difference between seeing the lights and watching them turn on for the first time." Eve tried to visualize it, hoping that would help her put the difference into words. "They turn off the streetlights, and most of the shops turn off their lights, too. It's probably the only few minutes of the year when Main Street is truly dark. Then there's no countdown or anything so you don't know exactly when it will happen, there's just anticipation. Everyone is quiet, just a few moments of giddy silence and then… an explosion of beautiful colors and cheering and yelling and music starts."

96

Ben said nothing at first. "I'm trying to remember how old I was the last time I... I don't remember the other lights going off or anything so dramatic. Is that new?"

"It's been that way as long as I can remember. But if you don't... it'll be like you're seeing the lights come on for the first time for the first time. And I'll see you seeing the lights for the first time for the first time." Eve pulsed with excitement. It'd be an amazing moment.

"I'm looking forward to it more than I was before I talked to you," Ben said.

The conversation began to feel intimate again, as though they spoke of something just the two of them would share rather than the whole town. Eve hadn't meant for that to happen. "Okay. I'll see you then," she said. She hung up feeling unsettled. She put the phone away and went upstairs to get ready for bed. A future conversation loomed in her head despite efforts to push it away. He wouldn't be crushed. He'd know it was right, probably even knew it was coming. She hoped her brother would understand as well.

She heard two other brothers making the expected noise as they entered the house. She and Drew used to make noise coming in together before he left for school. Now he didn't answer his phone when she called. But Thanksgiving wasn't a time to catch worries. Eve drifted to sleep trying to count blessings instead of sheep.

9

The delicious aroma of roasting turkey filled the house. The noise of family filled the house as well. An extra table had been placed at the end of the long one in the kitchen so that it stretched into the living room. Eve sat in the middle, near where the tables met, and swiveled her attention from one side to the other as the conversations ebbed and flowed.

At the far end, John was putting food in front of Spencer a few bites at a time to see what he liked while Anna ate with a sleeping baby in one arm. Grandpa Will was next to Anna and had just remarked that the sleeping baby reminded him of the time Dan tried to earn some money with a homework stand.

"He put a table out in the front yard with a sign that offered homework help for two dollars an hour for grades... How old were you when you did the homework stand?" Grandpa Will called down the table. "Eighth grade?"

Dan nodded but also rolled his eyes at hearing the story again.

"I think it was eighth grade. He was only offering help for grades six through eight because he thought younger kids wouldn't have any homework or money to pay for help with it." He tapped his temple to indicate he thought it was a smart strategy. "The sign also said he could help most with math because that was his specialty. The only customer he got was that little girl from down the street. What was her name?"

Dan shrugged, even though Eve was certain he remembered because she only knew the name from hearing him say it last time Grandpa told the story.

"Michelle," Eve supplied helpfully.

"Right. Michelle Townsend." Grandpa Will nodded as the name came to him. "That girl was sharp as a tack and didn't need any homework help. She just wanted to spend some time with Dan. It's no wonder, of course, since the boy got his looks from his old man." He paused to allow everyone a moment to appreciate his joke.

Eve chuckled with those around her.

Tori leaned over and whispered, "He's actually quite dashing in his wedding photos."

Eve silently agreed. She refrained from saying anything about the fact she thought Simon now looked a lot like those pictures. He was sitting across the table and wouldn't appreciate it.

"Little Michelle Townsend came by every day after school for almost two weeks," Grandpa Will said.

"It was three days," Dan muttered.

Grandpa Will likely didn't hear the correction, but he would have continued as though he hadn't either way. "Dan eventually figured out he wasn't the brilliant tutor he thought he was. He wanted to return the girl's money when he realized she didn't need his help, but he thought that might embarrass her, or himself just as much. So he simply closed down his enterprise and hid from her."

Dan cleared his throat as though he might have something to say to that. He said nothing.

"It was for the best," Noah said. "He made a much better choice in the end." He smiled at his mom, who was sitting on a couch next to Eve's mom, both women eating from plates in their laps.

She smiled back with her eyes narrowed enough to let him know she recognized the comment as false flattery.

"Suck up," Sarah joked quietly.

She was next to Noah and right across from Eve. They might've been the only two who heard her.

Eve might have thought that Sarah coming to the family Thanksgiving with Noah confirmed that they were in a relationship except that it was the third Thanksgiving that Tori had joined Simon, and those two still insisted they were only friends.

"You know what that reminds me of… slacks." He stopped talking to take a bite of stuffing. He seemed to chew for a long time, especially considering the consistency of stuffing. Then he took another bite.

James was pinching his lips together to keep from laughing out loud.

Eve didn't know if her grandpa was waiting for someone to ask what he meant, wasn't going to tell the story most of them already knew – which seemed least likely since that never stopped him before – or if he'd simply forgotten he was talking.

"What about slacks?"

"What reminds you of slacks?"

John and Matt had spoken at the same time. James gave up holding in the laugh and a tear leaked out at their questions.

Grandpa Will looked between them with amusement twinkling in his eyes. He'd clearly been waiting for a question and was delighted at getting two. He waved his fork towards Matt and said, "All of it." Then the fork pointed at John before waving to include the rest of the table. "When your mother was in high school, she had a couple of her girlfriends over, and *her* mother – your grandmother – came into the room holding a basket of laundry. She announced that she'd washed a few pairs of your mom's slacks to fill a load – your mom typically did her own washing – and asked where she'd like them. Your mom grabbed them and said, 'They're jeans, Mom,' before she put them away. Later, after her friends went home, she gave her mother an earful about how she'd never been more mortified in her life. I never did figure out what was wrong with the word slacks."

Several pairs of eyes turned towards Eve's mom. She shrugged and said, "Sometimes weird things embarrass you at that age. I think one of my friends kind of smirked at the word, and that was enough."

"Am I the only one hearing these stories for the first time?" Sarah asked. "Is that why I'm the only one who laughed at slacks?"

"I laughed," James said.

"You laugh whenever anyone says slacks," Eve said.

James snickered again to prove it. "No one says that word. It's funny."

"You're so lucky to have this awesome family," Tori said. She was smiling and sounded a bit sarcastic. But Eve had a feeling she was completely serious.

"Travis Shannon said he'd lead the games at the Christmas Festival," Simon said, somewhat out of nowhere.

"What *reminded* you of Christmas?" Matt joked.

101

"Mom was looking at me," he said. "I knew she was dying to ask me how the planning is coming."

"I wasn't going to ask."

"She was," James said.

"And you... um..."

Eve laughed as her mom crammed a bite in her mouth to keep from finishing her sentence, but her body was still tense from the mention of the last name. Travis Shannon was Ben's father. Simon had been talking to him? Would he say anything about Ben? Eve glanced at Tori. She wanted to ask if she'd told Simon that Ben had been there helping her paint. But why would it matter if she didn't have anything to hide? She cast her eyes around in search of a topic that would distract her from uncomfortable thoughts and uncomfortable possibilities.

"The flowers are so pretty, Sarah," she said. "Thanks again for bringing them."

Sarah smiled at the praise as several people echoed Eve. Sarah had brought four small mason jars with red, yellow and orange flowers spilling out the tops. They were spaced along the table so everyone could enjoy one fairly close.

"Are they real?" James asked as he fingered a flower and pulled off a petal. "Oops."

"Real flowers do tend to be more fragile," Anna said.

"Of course they're real," Noah said. "Did you really think a *florist* would bring fake flowers?" He sounded offended on Sarah's behalf.

James put on a contrite expression. "Like I know anything about flowers. These seem too perfect to be real."

"Until you ripped it apart," Matt said.

"It was one petal!"

102

Sarah appeared to be convincing Noah that the question hadn't bothered her. The defense that they looked too perfect to be real probably helped. A few conversations sprang up at once, some about the flowers and some about the food. Eve watched Spencer holding a fork in one hand and picking up food with the other. John was trying to instruct him on using the fork, but it wasn't going well. Spencer kept waving the fork as though holding it was success. Eve enjoyed some of the cranberry sauce she'd made. Listening for the berries to pop had been fun. She heard snippets of conversation about football teams she didn't care about and whether or not cornbread improved stuffing until her name caught her full attention.

"You know what this reminds me of... Eve."

She turned to her grandpa at the same time she realized he wasn't talking *to* her but was on the verge of a story *about* her. His stories were generally more entertaining when they were centered on other family members, but she still didn't expect anything terribly cringey.

"The girl has always been an excellent helper for her mom, sometimes even trying to take care of her older brothers."

John laughed. "Oh, yeah. For almost a year, I had her convinced it was easier for her to get the fitted sheet on my bed because she was shorter, and I had to lean over more to do it."

Eve frowned at that memory.

"You're shorter than me now," Matt said. "Can I get you to make my bed?"

"No," Eve said. "I'm not seven anymore."

"Yeah, she smartened up eventually," John said.

Someone at the other end of the table mumbled something about whether or not smartened was a real word.

Grandpa Will picked up the story he'd started. "She must have been only five or six because Matt was a newborn. She wanted to help feed him so bad she found a bottle and filled it with who knows what. She had it in the baby's mouth before her mom came and stopped her."

"You tried to poison me!?" Matt was only playfully shocked since he was obviously unharmed.

Eve was genuinely shocked because she couldn't believe she hadn't heard the story before.

"It was just milk." Eve's mom cut into various surprised voices with a cool tone. "He was only two months old and not supposed to be having cow's milk yet, but a few sips would not have poisoned him. He was refusing the bottle anyway."

"I guess I was born smartened." Matt grinned with mock pride. It would have earned him more eye rolls if he'd been serious.

"Is it time for dessert?" Eve's dad turned hopeful eyes towards his wife.

Eve looked that direction as well. She was ready.

A nod met all the looks. "Guests should stay seated. Eve is still very helpful, and the two of us can bring out the pies."

Eve took her cue to begin clearing away most of the plates, Simon and Anna were still eating from theirs, while her mom set her fancy scalloped-edge dessert plates in front of everyone over the age of two. The pies would be passed around with serving utensils for each person to cut the size he wanted. The pie Grandpa Will brought started with him.

"I'll cut myself a very small slice so there's enough to go around," he said. "I know you all want to try some of my famous pumpkin pie."

Eve and Tori shared a smile before he even said it.

"It's so famous they put the recipe right on the side of the can."

"I still think we ought to offer some sort of dessert pizza," Noah said.

"No work talk away from work," Dan said.

"Let me take an informal survey that has nothing to do with the restaurant." Noah glanced around the room. "What's everyone's favorite dessert pizza?"

"Chocolate," Tori said.

At least two other voices repeated that preference.

"I'm not sure," Anna said, "but probably some sort of fruit. Cherry or strawberry maybe."

"Yeah, that sounds good."

"It sounds like pie, not pizza," Dan said.

"Don't some people call it pizza pie?"

Dan shook his head. "Not mine they don't."

Eve briefly considered posting that the word pie had been banned, but that wouldn't fit the theme.

"Maybe chocolate and cherry?" John suggested. "Like with some of that super sweet filling in a chocolate-covered cherry."

Noah's eyes widened.

"I didn't see a chocolate pie." Grandpa Will scanned the table for the dessert he thought he missed.

"Not here," John said. "We're talking about a possible dessert for Pans and Plates."

"No, we're not," Noah said quickly. "We're just talking about dessert pizzas people like. If I happen to get inspired, we'll talk about that later when we're at work."

"I can't wait," Dan muttered dryly.

"You're making pies at the restaurant now?" Grandpa Will asked. Fortunately for Dan, he didn't wait for an answer before he said, "Pie reminds me of laundry."

Eve wasn't sure she wanted to know if there was an actual connection there. Her brain immediately conjured an odd picture of a neat lattice-topped pie spinning around at the bottom of a washing machine.

Simon caught her eye. "Why do you look surprised that pie reminds Grandpa of anything?"

She only laughed rather than try to explain the weirdness it put unbidden into her head. Grandpa Will told the story of the first time he did laundry, trying to help out his wife when their first child was a baby. He overflowed the washing machine because he thought he needed to fill it with buckets of water before he turned it on. He got louder and more animated as he described and mimed trying to hide water all over the floor from his wife. The laundry room was at the back of that house, and he – according to him – opened the door and bailed water outside like he was trying to keep a boat from sinking.

Then he used all the rag rugs in the house to mop up the floor and hung them all on the line. There wasn't room for all the clothes he was washing. He let his wife believe he decided to wash all the rugs, too, and failed to plan ahead for space on the line. That was somehow preferable to admitting he didn't know how to use a washing machine.

"She figured out I didn't know how to wash rugs though, complained about having to wash them properly herself, so I might've lost whatever points I got for washing the clothes." He pushed his plate back. "And just recounting that fiasco took it out of me. I'm in danger of falling asleep at this table."

"This is later than we usually have lunch," Anna said. "It's getting past Spencer's nap time, too."

The gathering broke into the commotion of ending. John and Anna took their kids home to nap before meeting her parents for dinner. They joked that they wouldn't need to eat for a week after two Thanksgiving meals in one day. Simon drove Grandpa Will home, and Tori left at the same time. Sarah was taking Noah to dinner with her family. They left holding hands, which finally gave Eve the information she'd been seeking.

Dan and Aunt Stacy stayed to watch football. Eve and her mom were not big fans. Though they checked in on the game occasionally, they also got the house cleaned up and ready for the decorations they'd pull out the next day.

10

$\mathcal{E}$ve wondered how Goldilocks would have survived a
longer story. She'd spent over an hour sitting on furniture
that was too hard, too soft, too big, too scratchy and too stiff. And
that didn't include any of the couches she didn't even try because
they were too ugly, too weird, too pointy and too that many shades
of orange should never be in one place.

The trip had been surprisingly disappointing. Eve had
expected to be overwhelmed with choices. She thought she'd come
home with a list of couches and measurements and prices and
spend a lot of time staring at her list not knowing what to do. She
did not expect to find nothing she liked.

Eve reminded herself that she'd made progress by painting
the room, then she tried not to let the trip bring her down while she
helped her mom put some Christmas lights on the porch and had
dinner with her family. Then she set out for the meeting at St.
Jude's. She spotted Noah walking with Sarah, Jackson and Cassidy
as she got out of her car. They were nearly a block away so she
waved rather than wait for them. Sarah was holding Noah's hand
again. Eve smiled as she opened the door. She was happy for her
cousin.

The little kids were already playing in the hallway, something that seemed to involve singing several different tunes at the same time. Eve said hello to the group. One kid waved back and both of the adults smiled and said, "Hello." The other kids acted as though they didn't see her. The room was buzzing with chatter.

"Hi, Eve!" Emily's voice registered above the noise more because of the name than the volume. There was a seat next to her, which Eve claimed.

"Hi," she said. "Did you have a good Thanksgiving?"

"I ate too much, but I gave myself permission because of the holiday. Although I must still feel guilty or I wouldn't be thinking about it so much." Emily was clearly speaking to Eve, but she mostly faced the baby trying to stand on her lap and used overly happy inflection to entertain him.

"Me, too. On all counts," Eve said.

"Me, three," Heather said.

Commiserating smiles passed between the ladies in the room.

Cassidy came in with Jackson and claimed seats on the other side of the room. Ben was with Noah and Sarah when they came in. Eve only noticed out of the corner of her eye since she'd started making faces at Emily's baby who was laughing in response. The baby kept giggling while various voices discussed turkey and gravy and pie. Noah and Ben were talking about Grandpa Will's famous pie.

"Okay, everyone, I guess we'll get started." Gabriel offered a prayer for a fruitful meeting with gratitude that so many people were able to gather. Then he led the guys across the hall.

Eve saw Ben laughing at something Noah said before she put her eyes back on closing the circle of ladies. Ruth was excited to start talking about Advent even though it wasn't Advent yet. She

109

had some questions inspired by St. Cecelia, the patron of musicians. Her first question was whether or not Christmas carols were appropriate during Advent.

"Some people," she said, "would say that we shouldn't skip over the waiting to the celebration."

"Some Christmas songs aren't particularly celebratory," Jessica said. "Mary Did You Know comes to mind."

"That's still about the baby though," Cassidy said. "A song doesn't really have to be... bouncy or upbeat to be... uh... jubilant."

"Is there a difference between a Christmas song and a Christmas carol?" Heather asked. "Because if it's not exactly... um... liturgical, does it matter if we listen to it during Advent?"

"In my opinion, there are some Christmas songs we shouldn't listen to ever." Emily punctuated her statement with an exaggerated expression of disgust that made her baby squeal.

Several people started to talk at once. Ruth quickly raised both her hands to get everyone's attention and said, "Wait!"

The room was startled into silence.

"No names," she said. "No song names, I mean. If we start talking about specific Christmas songs, someone is going to say she doesn't like my favorite."

"Are you saying you have a weird favorite?" Sarah asked.

"Just that some people don't appreciate it, and... Well, mostly I think we'll get super sidetracked if we start listing songs we like and different versions and..." Ruth shrugged uncertainly.

"If we can go back to Heather's question about the difference between songs and carols," Jessica said, "I think carols have religious significance, more like hymns."

110

"But if it's a carol, does that mean we can't sing it during Advent?" Eve asked. She loved singing Christmas carols all through December. And maybe some of November. January wasn't out of the question, though it was out of Advent.

"Not necessarily," Jessica said.

"I don't think the church has an official restriction," Cassidy said, "but I have heard some people say you shouldn't sing too early if... like how do we keep Advent separate?"

"Those are probably the same people who say you have to wait until Christmas Eve to put up a tree," Heather said.

"Probably."

"I like that the church isn't decorated before Christmas," Tori said. "But I think houses are different."

"Decorating can be a way to prepare."

"Unless it's skipping the work of Advent."

"The work?" Ruth said.

"Work might not be the best word." Cassidy paused to consider what she was trying to say. "Have you made some effort to reflect on the importance of what the holiday celebrates or are you jumping to the fun and making it all frivolous?"

"The songs do help me prepare," Eve said. "I think... I think when I sing Christmas songs, I'm thinking about how exciting it is that it's *coming*, not that it's here. Some lyrics are deep and... but I won't try to get specific because we aren't doing that."

Several ladies smiled at her quick disclaimer. There were a few lyric snippets mentioned about a weary world, poor shepherds and one Latin phrase they all knew before Heather shared a link to a game where they could try to guess carols by random lyrics. Then Ruth said she knew they'd got lost in the weeds and steered the conversation to how much to decorate during Advent. Some favorite traditions were shared and some ways people decorated a little at a time to build up to Christmas. The meeting ended with light reminders that Advent still didn't start for a few days so they all had plenty of time to get it "right."

Not everyone was going to the town lighting, but Eve knew that Emily was taking her kids. She followed her out and got to hold the youngest while Joseph loaded some toys and pulled a double stroller out of the back of their van. Eve continued to hold the little boy while Emily pushed her bigger but still little kids in the stroller. She was aware that Ben was talking to Joseph on the sidewalk behind them. She heard bits of the conversation about Joseph's Gym and Ben sounded engaged. It was possible and even likely that his place in the crowd had nothing to do with positioning himself near Eve.

Emily chatted about all the lights she'd put in the front window of the gym and about wanting to let her oldest flip the switch. She wasn't sure the little one would do it fast enough, and she wasn't sure she had the patience not to jump in if there was a delay. When they reached Main Street, Joseph took his son from Eve and led his family off to do their part.

Ben stepped up next to Eve. "No matter what, this'll be more fun than what Nate's doing right now."

Eve laughed. "I'm sorry to say I wish you'd have lost the bet so I could hear all about putting up lights with your mom."

He shook his head and jokingly called her a sadist. "So you're the expert," he said. "Where is a good spot to watch all this?"

"If you want hot chocolate, you want to be on the other side of the street because everyone over there is already in line, and you'll never get some otherwise." She was kidding. Though the line was long, most of the crowd wasn't part of it. "I like to stand

112

in front of Burger Brothers. It's in the middle of the block so you can see the lights all around, and the crowd is thinner there than trying to get a good view of the stage."

"I guess that makes sense if we aren't staying for the music anyway." He motioned for Eve to lead the way.

No longer holding a warm baby, Eve stuffed her hands into her coat pockets as he fell into step next to her. She was trying not to appear troubled by his words. *We* aren't staying for the music? She thought back to their conversation about the event. She'd encouraged him to go, but there was nothing that sounded like making plans together. Ben must only have meant he agreed with her disinterest in the music.

"Eve!"

She jumped at the sound of her name. She'd nearly walked past Simon on a bench without even seeing him. "Oh, hi," she said.

His eyes swept curiously over Ben before returning to his sister. "Have you seen Mom or Grandpa Will?"

"No, but I just got here," Eve said. "We came straight from the church." It felt important to let Simon know Ben was with her because they came from the same place.

Simon nodded. He glanced at his phone.

"Are you meeting them here?"

"I think so." Simon looked up and down the street. "I got a coherent as usual text from Grandpa that I thought was asking me to pick him up. But then I talked to Mom. She said she was bringing him but didn't sound entirely sure. I told her I'd save the bench in front of my place for him, which is the *only* reason I'm sitting here."

Eve smiled at his defensive tone. She wondered if he'd actually gotten a comment or just didn't like how it looked to be a healthy young man taking up one of only a handful of benches in a crowd. Some people had brought their own chairs though. Those were all set up closer to the corner.

"I wasn't going to say anything about it," she said. "Tori left the church just ahead of me. I'm surprised she hasn't found you. Maybe she's with Mom and Grandpa." Eve looked around for any sign of any of those people. She turned back when she failed.

Simon was staring at her with a strange and unreadable expression. He was quiet so long she started to think he might be upset with her for… mentioning Tori?

"She went to get a blanket," he said finally.

"Okay." Eve wasn't going to say anything about the tense moment either. "If I see Grandpa Will, I'll send him your way."

Simon had returned his eyes to his phone, but he nodded at her words.

Eve mumbled to Ben as they moved on. "I'm not sensing Christmas spirit there."

"I'm sure he'll brighten up when he finds everyone."

"Yeah." Eve remembered Simon saying he didn't have any interest in the town lighting. He was probably only there because of those other people. It made sense he'd be happier when they were with him.

The streetlights turned off, and a ripple of excited murmurs moved up and down the street.

"Things are happening already?" Ben said.

"This will be a good spot. We can even see Joseph's Gym from here." Eve planted her feet with the striped awning of Burger Brothers just ahead and turned to face the street.

114

Ben rubbed his hands together at her side. His gloves made a rustling sound. "Explain this to me now," he said. "What are we hoping to see?"

"Christmas lights!"

He smiled at her enthusiastic non-answer. "What makes them special tonight when we'll be seeing them all month?"

A light turned off in a window near them.

"When they're on, they're just on," she said. "That's nice of course, but watching them come on is more of an event. So... when the streetlights went off, that was the signal for the businesses to start turning their lights off. They try not to do it all at once so it takes longer, more buildup. There's one." She pointed across the street where another light had turned off.

Ben had seen it. "They really turn off all the lights? Even the businesses that are open?"

"Enough that it does get very dark," Eve said. "I think there's someone down at that corner who won't participate. I don't know why. And there are probably a few small lights left on where it might be unsafe otherwise. Last year, I could hear Chip commanding everyone to stay seated while his lights were out." She smiled at the memory. Chip owned Burger Brothers and was incredibly intimidating. But when she'd been outside, out of the line of fire for his commands, they'd been surprisingly amusing. "He said he warned everybody, and they had their chance to leave. No complaining was allowed from anyone who didn't take his advice."

"Um... I..." Ben cast a wary eye towards that awning. "What happens after it's dark?"

"Well... it'll stay dark for maybe ten minutes. I think that's to let everyone's eyes adjust and so we don't know exactly when it'll

115

happen. And then that tree on the stage will be the first thing. There's a whole nomination process for who gets to do that, and I didn't hear who it'll be this year and anyway… Once the tree lights up, someone turns on all those lights around the poles and up there, and all the businesses turn on what they've hung. The lights go on much faster than they turn off, and we all clap and cheer."

A small group of people rushed past on the sidewalk. Eve and Ben stepped closer to the building to give them room. Eve felt a strong impulse to grab Ben's hand so she didn't lose him in the growing darkness. It was a ridiculous impulse because she knew it wouldn't be *that* dark. And once the group passed, they had plenty of space and no risk of being jostled apart. Her hands remained firmly in her pockets.

"What happens to the tree?" Ben asked.

She saw him clearly despite the dim lighting, traced his familiar profile with her eyes, noticed that even though she wasn't holding on, he was still close enough that their sleeves brushed.

He was looking at the tree on the stage. The street was barricaded at both ends of the block with a temporary stage erected at one end. Eve took a small step back to focus on the confusing question. She'd already explained what happened to the tree. "It lights up first," she said.

"No, I mean after tonight. It can't stay in the middle of the street once the stage is gone, and I don't remember seeing a tree like that downtown last year."

The stage would need to come down to reopen the street. Eve knew there hadn't been a tree near that corner in the past. "I don't know," she said.

Ben shrugged as though it didn't matter.

116

It didn't matter, but it still bugged Eve. "I can't believe I never… I'm sure I've watched them light up a tree on that stage at least ten times, and it never occurred to me that it disappeared after tonight. Why not put the tree somewhere it can stay? Why are we lighting up something that isn't really part of the decorations? Why is my town doing something weird, and how have I never noticed before that it's weird?"

"I'm sorry I ruined it for you." Ben said it through a laugh that made his voice and his shoulders shake. He did not look or sound sorry.

Eve put aside her dramatics, for the moment. She was going to talk to her family later to see if any of them noticed the abandoned tree. "Stop laughing so you'll be prepared to cheer appropriately."

"I'm expected to cheer *appropriately*?"

"If you don't want to really ruin it for me." She narrowed her eyes playfully at him.

He'd stopped laughing, but he was still amused. "What level of cheering do you consider appropriate? Is this like a golf clap or more like the last round of the Stanley Cup?"

"It's just a pick-up game at the park, but Nate has the ball and his team is down by one."

Ben's eyebrows shot up. "That is a very specific level of cheering. I don't know if I can match that to, uh, lights."

"Oh, I have faith in you," Eve said.

Something flashed in his eyes at her teasing, something that went beyond amusement, something she tried not to think about or even fully notice. Fortunately, a Christmas tree lit up over his shoulder. Eve pointed. More lights came on around them.

Ben clapped with her and yelled, "Go, lights!" with mock enthusiasm. His eyes bounced to the various displays with obvious appreciation as they lit up though. Eve didn't mind that the cheering was only for her benefit. He did join in as everyone, or most everyone, sang "We Wish You a Merry Christmas."

After that, some guy on the stage tried to do a jazzy version of "Frosty the Snowman." Eve didn't feel tempted to stay longer to listen. "I think that's my cue to call it a night," she said.

"I'll walk you back to the church."

She led them across the street first to get a better look at some of the lights on that side. On one window, someone had cut out snowflakes and taped fairy lights behind them. The paper was pale blue and the lights had a cool cast that made Eve shiver as she approached it. The window was framed with a string of shiny holly. "I like this one," she said.

Ben nodded and then tipped his head back to the other side of the street. "Looks like Simon found everyone."

"And then some," Eve said.

Grandpa Will was on the bench with Tori. They were surrounded by Simon, Eve's parents and brothers, a couple of their friends and Noah's brother and his wife as well.

"Should we cross here?"

Eve shook her head. "If we stop to chat, we'll never leave." That was a good reason, even if it wasn't the only reason she wanted to avoid her family. They crossed at the end of the block as Ben asked how her shopping trip turned out.

"It didn't," Eve said. "I looked at so many things I didn't like. I wish I could say I was at least ruling stuff out, but I don't think that's how it works."

"Are you always so picky?" Ben said lightly.

"No!" She gave him a poke with her elbow for suggesting it. "I'm not being picky. I just can't seem to find who sells good couches."

He asked her to describe some of the bad couches. He said bad couches as though it was surrounded with air quotes, and yet he nodded understandingly as she explained the ones with rough or scratchy fabric and the ones that were too deep to use the backrest without practically lying down and the ones with ugly colors and the one with rock-hard armrests where she'd smacked her funny bone as she sat down.

"Okay. I think I'm convinced you're not actually picky," Ben said. "I think you just had really bad luck. I bet if you try a different store, you'll find something more promising."

"Not for a while. I mean, I think I need time to recover from all the sitting on uncomfortable furniture."

"Time to recover?" He laughed, which was good because she was trying to be funny.

"Yes. From the sitting *and* the disappointment. It was awful." They were crossing the church parking lot, and Eve stopped at his car rather than continue on to hers. He'd walked her far enough.

"Well, if you're not furniture shopping this weekend, what are you doing?"

"I'm working tomorrow," Eve said. She wondered if she could avoid thinking about her yellow room on Sunday. Maybe she needed a break. Maybe if she avoided staring at it, inspiration would arrive unforced.

"Is there a chance you'd be willing to do something with me on Sunday?" Ben asked. "I could show you the latest house. It's almost finished. It just needs a few details, mostly in the kitchen."

119

Eve's mind was jumping around before he finished the question. It was a tempting offer, made even more tempting by the nerves that seemed to be behind his extra words. And that was exactly why she had to say no. She'd tried to avoid any question that would force her to clarify their relationship status by keeping their conversations focused on topics from the church group. How had she gotten so careless? Was there any way to say no and still leave the door open for him to ask again later without explicitly telling him to wait?

Ben had no idea what was going on in her head, but he could see the hesitation it produced. "That's okay. You don't have to say no. You can... we can pretend I didn't... try to forget anyway. Um..."

He was disappointed and trying to spare her feelings about having to disappoint him. That was sweet, too sweet. It made Eve feel guilty and awful, and she acted without thinking. She pushed up on her toes to kiss his cheek, then ran to her car. She didn't run because she thought Ben might chase her for an explanation but because she hoped she could somehow run faster than she could try to explain to herself. Did she really just kiss Ben Shannon? It wasn't a kiss kiss, just a quick peck like she might give a family member in a moment of gratitude or after having been apart for a while. She'd thought, if she could call it thinking at all, to offer a second of comfort. But Ben was not a family member, and he hadn't been looking for comfort. Eve was very careful not to look his direction as she drove away.

The house was quiet when she got home, which wasn't a surprise since she'd just seen almost everyone she knew downtown. She got ready for bed a bit early. A solid night of sleep could only improve her decision-making for the next day. Rather than sleeping, she ended up spending the long night asking herself questions she couldn't answer because she made the mistake of checking her phone one last time. Simon had texted. He said, "How did Ben not know you're engaged? That's not cool, sis."

11

$\mathcal{I}$t was easier than Eve expected to focus on work while she was at work. She had hope that she would eventually be able to explain everything to Ben. Maybe he'd understand. Since she couldn't even talk to him for several more days, it did her no good to dwell on it or the unpleasant conversation that had to happen first.

Noah was an excellent distraction. He'd apparently given up on the bows in favor of an even better, so he said, improvement to the Christmas pizza. But Dan had the day off, and Noah wouldn't tell anyone before he talked to his dad about it. He was just randomly saying, "It's gonna be awesome," in the middle of other conversations. Eve went home and posted that something was going to be awesome.

She spent more of Sunday thinking about all the couches she wasn't buying than she planned or wanted. Her break for inspiration would have to wait until she didn't have something else she wanted to think about even less.

Noah didn't work on Monday or Tuesday. By the time Eve went to Pans and Plates on Wednesday, her followers had amused her with quite a few guesses on what Noah expected to be awesome. Her favorites were probably the guy who suggested it was a pizza flambéed on your doorstep – who included an image of Dan's head on a guy with a flamethrower – and the guy who suggested the restaurant was going to be renamed Noah's Edible Ideas. She was curious to find out the real idea and was surprised to find out that Dan didn't know.

"I asked him after I saw some of the nonsense online," he said, "but Noah told me we shouldn't talk about work stuff at home because that's what I always say. Might be the first time I was ever annoyed that someone listened to me."

Eve smiled knowingly. "I bet he said it like he knew it would annoy you."

"That's it right there."

"Does anyone think this idea will live up to the hype?" Another employee was getting ready to slide a pizza into the oven.

"I don't think a few days of speculation qualifies as hype," Eve said.

Dan grunted and moved towards his office at the back. It was likely he had work there, and equally likely he was avoiding further discussion of the speculation.

The other employee, Madison, began to list all the ideas that had been mentioned to get Eve's opinion on which were even possible. She also wanted assurance that Eve would update everyone as soon as she found out since Madison wouldn't be there when Noah came in. She was a college student who had short shifts to accommodate her class schedule.

When Noah finally arrived, Dan was making a delivery. Eve greeted him casually without hinting that she was curious about anything. Noah took a minute to check the current orders and that everything was caught up, then set to work at the next table kneading a mound of dough.

"How's Sarah?" Eve asked.

"Selling flowers," he said, not looking up.

"That's what she's doing, not how she's doing."

"You don't really want to know how she's doing anyway. You only want to find out if I saw her or talked to her this morning."

That wasn't entirely fair. Sarah wasn't a close friend, but Eve liked her and was genuinely concerned about her welfare. Her question was more about finding out how the relationship was progressing though. She was grudgingly grateful that he called out her leaning towards sneaky gossip and changed her question to be more direct. "Did you see her?"

Noah paused a moment before he said, "She looked happy to see me."

Eve grinned and rewarded the response by not prying further. She was happy for him even with the uncertainty of her own prospects.

Dan returned. He hung up his coat and stood directly in front of Noah with his arms folded across his chest. He didn't say anything.

"First of all," Noah said, "I don't remember the last time we went so long without working together, and it's not my fault I happened to get a great idea at the same time. I'm not the one who tried to turn it into a big reveal."

Both guys looked pointedly at Eve.

She could only offer a shrug in her defense. "I didn't think I had until I spent an hour talking to Madison about it."

The guys silently turned back to each other. Eve was glad to be out from under their scrutiny.

"So I think you have to agree that Franks' Pizza has been one of my most successful innovations," Noah started.

Dan frowned. "Yes. And this better not be about changing it."

"No, no. I just brought it up to say part of what makes it great is involving another local business."

"And the other part is that it doesn't mess with my pizza."

"Hang on to that thought," Noah said. "This Christmas pizza is already expected next week, and I've been trying to come up with a way to package it special, packaging that doesn't interfere with the pizza itself."

Dan stayed quiet. He only motioned that Noah continued to have the floor.

"I was talking to Joseph Ziebert about what they're doing for Christmas. He said Emily came up with an idea to let the kids – and the parents if they want – draw Christmas pictures before or after class. Mostly it's something to do if they're early and waiting for class to start. They're displaying the pictures on the front window, and he was trying to figure out what to do when they run out of space because they've covered nearly half already. He was wondering about how long to rotate them or maybe ask if neighboring businesses would be willing to display some, and I thought... we could display them on pizza boxes!"

"How?" Dan was still frowning, and now he looked confused.

"Tape," Noah said. He managed to make it not sound totally obvious.

Dan sighed. "How would we keep track of the pictures? Even if they were numbered or something, it would be such a hassle to dig through a stack of pictures to find what goes with each order."

"I think you're trying to make it complicated, and it's not," Noah said.

"It's not complicated?" Dan walked away, which was his typical response when he needed to mull something over.

Noah turned to Eve. "You get it, right?"

"Maybe? You want to let kids decorate pizza boxes at Joseph's Gym and then order them here? That does sound a little… hard to track."

"People are not tracking this idea." Noah shook his head. "Let me try again. When anyone orders a Christmas pizza, they get a picture on the box, a random, whatever is on top of the stack of pictures picture. Joseph and Emily will make sure the kids know that no one's keeping track and there will only be a very small chance they'll end up with their own picture. I think kids would think it's fun to get a surprise picture. And telling them about it will help us advertise the Christmas pizza. In return – and this is where you come in – we'll make sure that customers know the pictures were drawn by kids at Joseph's Gym. It's a cross-promotion win-win."

"Now that you've simplified it, it's starting to sound fun," Eve said.

"It was never complicated."

Dan returned. He'd been close enough to listen and only took a few steps to reinsert himself in the conversation. "I agree that the less complicated version is promising."

"There's only one version," Noah said. He dropped the dough he'd been kneading and began to divide it into pizza-sized pieces.

"But we need to work out a few logistics and establish that under no circumstances are any of these pictures to contain glitter of any kind. I do not want that in my pizza."

Eve giggled at how emphatic he was. She didn't want glitter in her food either, but he said it as though he was banning Satan himself.

"Joseph is way ahead of you on that," Noah assured him. "He and Emily already had that discussion, and the gym is a glitter-free zone."

Dan nodded at Joseph's common sense, and they talked about when the pictures would be dropped off and whether it'd be better to tape them onto boxes ahead of time or not. Eve let her mind wander to how she could word the announcement when the temporary partnership was official. Maybe she could find some crayons and draw something to go with the post. She was no great artist so it might be fun to tease people that they could end up with her picture instead of something cute by a child. Or maybe…

Her mouth dropped open with the force of her fabulous idea, and her eyes darted from the sauce she was refilling to Dan.

"That's a terrifying expression." He held his hand up to stop her. "And I've already fielded one idea today." He moved purposefully away.

The phone rang so she couldn't even tell Noah her idea right away. It was perfect though. When Noah was free again, he asked if her idea was related to his idea.

"Yes! We get your dad to draw a picture for one of the boxes. First, I'll explain what's happening, how the Christmas pizzas will be decorated by kids. Then, right before it starts, I'll say that Dan got into the spirit and drew a picture, too! I'll post it with an announcement that someone will be lucky enough to get a box decorated by the Grinch himself."

Noah laughed. "I think that's a great idea, but you'll have a hard time getting my dad to go along with it."

"Really? You're usually pretty optimistic about talking him into things."

"How many of those things does he end up doing?" The question was rhetorical. They both knew his success rate was low. "And when I do, it takes a lot of convincing. You only have a few days to get him to cooperate. And off the top of my head, I can't remember a single time my dad has ever drawn a picture."

"Hmm." Eve would need to give her approach some thought. She wanted to surprise people with a picture by Dan. But would he be more likely to agree if she got enough followers requesting one?

A customer walked in, and Noah greeted him with, "It's gonna be awesome."

The guy was a regular who chuckled and knew better than to ask for clarification. He simply picked up his order and wished Noah luck.

Eve broached her idea with Dan shortly before she left for the day.

His only response was, "I'm not five."

She figured that meant she'd need more people involved in convincing him it was a good idea. Noah had been in touch with Joseph so the pictures were going to happen. Promoting that was her first priority, then she'd start nudging Dan to participate.

The empty yellow room bothered her more than usual when Eve got home. Memories of Ben helping her paint it felt different now. She also remembered her mom's concern from the same day that someone might be hurt. At the time, her friendship with Ben had seemed innocent. She knew it wasn't because she missed him too much, and she only missed him because she couldn't call him, couldn't try to explain yet. She'd done something wrong, but she didn't know how she could have done it right.

"Food," she whispered to herself to redirect her thoughts.

She retreated to the kitchen for some dinner with her family. The company and conversation helped more than relieving her hunger. Everyone agreed they'd like to see Dan decorate a pizza box. Matt and James had quite a few suggestions on what they'd like to see him draw. The best might have been a flock of flying reindeer delivering pizzas on their backs.

Eve returned to her empty room to post some replies and finally share the news of Noah's latest idea. But she refused to work sitting on the floor.

She went to a closet at the back of the house and pulled out a folding chair, then she got a throw pillow from her bedroom to make it more comfortable. Sitting on the pillow was awkwardly uneven, and it slid around when she tried to use it to cushion her back. She tossed it on the floor and concentrated on humorous replies and not which suggestions she wanted to ask Ben about.

One of her brothers poked his head into the room a bit later. "All your suffering over furniture for this room and you ended up with a folding chair and a lacy pillow?"

If the pillow had been closer, she'd have picked it up to throw at Matt. Instead, she matched his sarcasm with her own. "Yeah, it's perfect."

He smiled. "Tell Drew to bring home Simon's basketball so he'll give me the green one."

"Oh, my goodness. Why are these basketballs still an issue? I swear I'm going to buy you all a bunch of different colored ones for Christmas just so no one ever has to look for one."

"That'd be cool," he said, as though she'd been serious.

Maybe she would seriously consider it. "I'll tell him, but I'm still not your messenger."

"You are if you tell him." Matt ducked around the corner to ensure that was the last word.

Someone had already responded with excitement about getting the kids at Joesph's Gym to draw pictures. Eve swiped that away before she got sucked into a whole conversation. She dialed her brother.

"Hi, Drew. You know, sometimes it feels like you're mad at me when you never answer. But today I just want to say Matt wants you to bring home Simon's basketball and that doesn't really feel like something to answer the phone for. See you soon."

She exhaled sharply. Why had she said that about him being mad? Was she projecting fears for the future? More importantly, would he suspect she was doing that? It probably didn't matter this close to him coming home.

Eve called Aiden next. He did answer.

"Hi. I guess it's Wednesday."

"When was the last time you played basketball?"

"Uh… like a real game or just shooting by myself?"

"Either," Eve said. "When was the last time you did anything that used a basketball?"

"I've been kind of focused on studying so it's been at least a week. I should try to move some before the drive."

"Your last final is tomorrow, right? Then you're coming home Friday?"

"Actually, Drew's last final got bumped to the morning," Aiden said. "We'll both be done by noon so we're going to go ahead and leave tomorrow."

"Oh. It'll be nice to see you in person again. We can really talk."

"Yeah," he said. "Uh… yeah."

It sounded as though he sensed something ominous in her tone. Eve hadn't intended it to sound ominous. All the waiting would be for nothing if she tipped her hand over the phone. "And play a game or two maybe. That's something hard to do long distance. Matt was just bragging about how long his *Clank!* record has stood. You and Drew probably have the best chance at beating it."

"I haven't played *Clank!* since the summer. Definitely looking forward to that."

She asked him to remind her which class was the last final and chatted a bit about the possibility of snow slowing the drive. They were only expecting an inch or two, which wasn't enough to worry Drew, but it would make parents nervous.

Eve felt a weird mix of sadness and relief as she set down her phone. With Aiden about to visit, that might be her last Wednesday call with him. She picked up the phone a minute later to call Tori. If she did nothing but stare at the bare wall, her mind was going to torture her with memories of Ben painting it.

131

"How's your Christmas shopping going?" Tori said as she answered.

"Oh, um… I haven't even started yet." Eve didn't count the half-joking comment about basketballs.

"I only have Simon left. Do you have any ideas for him?"

"Not yet. And I'll probably need to use my first idea myself."

"Oh, you're so selfish," Tori teased.

Eve laughed with her. "Shouldn't Simon be easy for you? I mean, you guys have been… uh, friends a long time."

The line was silent a long time as Tori seemed to debate how to answer. Eve was kicking herself for the slip. She knew Tori didn't like having to correct people on the status of her relationship with Simon, and she'd stopped herself from saying they'd been "together." But Tori had likely caught what she'd almost said.

Finally, Tori said, "It's difficult because every year Simon tries to convince me I shouldn't get him anything, and I know he says that mostly because he doesn't want to have to get me something. But I *like* giving presents, and I always tell him that doesn't mean he has to get me one."

Eve knew that Simon wasn't just avoiding getting Tori a present. He didn't like shopping any more than most of the guys she knew. Eve was going to give a little something to each of her brothers even though she expected Drew to be the only one to give her something. Everyone was fine with that. She supposed it would be different with friends than with family. "I'll tell him to stop being difficult even though he won't listen to me," Eve said. "Guys can be pretty annoying sometimes."

"Yes. Totally. Thank you for trying to help." Tori sighed through the phone. "So anyway, I keep thinking I could get him something for his apartment because, I mean, this is the first year he has his own place. But all I can think of are like decorative things that I doubt he'd ever use. I actually considered a nice tablecloth for special occasions."

"He's still coming here for holidays and such," Eve said.

"Exactly," Tori agreed. "And I also thought about some sort of artwork or… he has nothing on the walls. But I know he'd hang it up even if he hated it, and I hate to think of him thinking of me every time he looks at some picture he thinks is awful."

"Yeah."

"I've tried really hard to come up with something that would have some use, but I'm coming up empty."

"Hmm. I don't know either."

"What if I give you a minute?" Tori said. "I kind of hoped if I talked you through my lame ideas, you'd be like… what about this great thing?"

Eve laughed at that hope, especially given her current circumstances. "I am absolutely the last person to ask about home décor. You know how long I've been trying to do something with the room I'm in right now… and I have literally furnished it with a folding chair and a throw pillow. The pillow is on the floor."

Tori started laughing with her. "I don't know, Eve. I think something is going on with you and that room."

"What do you mean?"

"Well, it's just… you normally strike me as an intelligent young woman who generally knows what she wants and yet… there must be some kind of mental block on that room."

"A mental block?" Eve repeated. "That would kind of make sense because I know it shouldn't be as hard as it is. But it doesn't make sense because I have no idea what could possibly be, I don't know, blocking me."

Tori didn't have any specific insights either. She did have more suggestions on what might be fun for Dan to draw, including elves making pizzas and a nativity scene with a glowing pizza replacing the star. She and Eve laughed uncomfortably as they wondered if that was cute or sacrilegious.

Eve managed to end the call without asking what happened last Friday. She knew that Ben had to have gone back downtown after she left in order to have talked to Simon. She was dying to know if there had been an embarrassing scene or only a quiet question. She didn't ask. Tori probably would have mentioned anything that seemed like a big deal. Eve mostly put it out of her head while she watched the end of a movie with her parents before bed. The main character made an emotional speech in front of a crowd that could have easily waited five minutes to happen in private. Eve felt a small measure of comfort that nothing in her life was that bad.

$\mathcal{D}$rew arrived later than expected. He quickly assured everyone that the roads weren't bad. He'd only gotten a later start than planned. He had dropped Aiden off to see his parents, but they'd already made plans for him to join the Donnellys for dinner the next day.

Eve avoided eye contact when he said Aiden was looking forward to seeing everyone. If he looked to see how happy she was or suspected she was nervous, she didn't want to know that. There wasn't much time for talking the night he arrived, and it was mostly filled with Drew answering questions about his classes.

Her younger brothers had school on Friday, and her dad went to work. Eve's mom agreed to a game she didn't particularly like and used it as an opportunity to pry into Drew's love life. He'd been spending a lot of time with someone named Mary Catherine. Though his answers were short, he barely avoided smiling with everything he said about her. Eve decided not to be terribly upset with this girl if she was partly to blame for how rarely Drew answered calls from his sister. Mary Catherine probably had more interesting things to talk about than a green basketball.

Susanna was making dinner. A delicious chicken scent slipped inside when Eve's dad returned from checking on her that evening. "I just saw Aiden pull up," he said.

James rushed to let him in before he could knock. Aiden was a big guy, over six feet and fairly broad. He was also a hugger. While Eve knew he wasn't trying to tackle any of the guys in her family, she was still somewhat surprised they were all still standing when he was done. She and her mom got gentler versions that lifted them off the ground rather than threatening to drop them to it. Eve didn't know where to look as she greeted him. Avoiding eye contact would be shifty, staring too long might convey her need to say something she couldn't say in front of everyone.

They were still in the midst of the preliminary greetings of asking after Aiden's parents and if he was glad to be home when Simon showed up. He survived a hug and then couldn't wait for everyone to give him input on a new song. He played three different versions. As usual, he needed to explain the subtle variations before anyone could give an opinion on which was best. The discussion was interrupted by another knock.

John and Anna came for dinner to welcome Drew home as well. Drew and Aiden fawned over the new baby they hadn't yet seen in person. Spencer wiggled out of his coat and ran towards the back door. Eve found him by the hooks, holding up his coat to see who was going to pick him up so he could reach one. He smiled when he saw her coming and held up the coat higher. She lifted him past her shoulders before bringing him level with the hooks.

When Eve set him back on the ground, he ran towards his mom. Eve waited where she was because she knew he'd be back with another coat to hang. He tripped over Anna's coat on his way, but he landed on it, and it was soft. Then he tried to pick it up

136

while he was still standing on it. Eve shared a smile with Anna, who was watching the adorable struggle, too.

Spencer eventually got the coat to Eve. She helped him get a grip on just the hood before she lifted him along the row of hooks until he snagged one. By the time they got John's coat on a hook, it was time to eat.

Having the older guys back at the table felt both familiar and foreign to Eve. The discussion of sports trades and some obscure rules were similar to ones that had played out at the same table countless times as she was growing up. Yet it looked different as these were adults and not boys. Even Matt spoke with a deep voice now. Eve mostly listened and found it all entertaining.

Simon wanted to share the song more after dinner. Eve had already given her opinion so she slipped into her dining room that might never be anything else to try to gather her thoughts. She knew she needed to talk to Aiden alone as soon as possible, yet she still didn't know what exactly to say.

Aiden followed her. "It's more yellow than I expected," he said.

"Too yellow?"

He shook his head. "It's not bad. I pictured something fainter, but I like it."

"Do you like how I've decorated it?" She gestured to her folding chair. She'd returned the pillow to her bed.

Aiden laughed at her sarcasm. "It's a start, I guess."

The music in the other room got louder as Simon tried to illustrate something. That was probably sufficient privacy, and there was already awkward tension in the room that would only get worse the longer she stalled. Eve plunged into a real conversation.

"I think we need to talk about how maybe we rushed into something that isn't really working out."

He didn't flinch at her bluntness, didn't appear surprised either. "Are you... wanting to... not be engaged or not be together at all?"

The words could have been sad. Aiden's tone was purely curious. Eve felt as though he wanted to know exactly what she was saying before he reacted at all. She'd been certain he would agree with her – that he saw it coming and already knew it'd be best – right up until she was faced with saying it out loud. Now she worried he was hiding his shock. She worried he'd be upset. For months, she'd hoped this conversation – while uncomfortable – would let them clear the air and return to the way things used to be. That hope suddenly felt naïve and impossible. But she couldn't say nothing. Going on as though the relationship was fine would be dishonest. "I, um... I think... we're better as friends. I think that's what God wants for us."

"So... *you're* breaking up with *me*?"

Eve was berating herself for mentioning God. It was true she'd poured a lot of prayer into the decision and true that she felt peace about it. But bringing God into the conversation felt as though she was telling Aiden he should blame the Almighty and not her if he didn't like it. Cringing over what she hadn't meant to say was what kept Eve from noticing at first the tremendous amount of relief in his voice. It caught up to her after a moment. "Uh... you sound like you wanted me to say that," she said.

"Not *wanted* exactly, but..." He smiled gently. "Expected?"

"You knew this wasn't working. Were you about to break up with me if I didn't do it first?"

"Oh, no way," he said quickly. "Your brothers would pound me."

Eve burst out laughing. The statement seemed ridiculous partly because her brothers were not the fighting type and partly because Aiden was bigger than any of them. Though realistically he couldn't take on all five at once, and Simon did have impressive biceps. Mostly she laughed to release the tension. She sobered quickly because despite the lack of physical threat, she understood how he'd worry about damaging his friendships, especially with Drew. Eve wasn't looking forward to telling Drew about the breakup either.

"So you were waiting for me to be the one to do it?"

"I needed to be able to say this was your decision."

"How long have you been waiting?"

"I was surprised you didn't say something before I went back to school."

Eve nodded because she should have said something then. She wished she'd had the nerve. During the pause, one line of Simon's new song was repeating over and over from the other part of the house. It only partially covered some of the comments about it being enough. Aiden rolled his eyes at how familiar that was. Maybe they couldn't really go back but the way forward was feeling passable.

"Is there anything you want to say to me before this is officially over?" Eve asked.

He shook his head slowly and scrunched up his eyes as though he was confused by the question.

Eve was a little confused by it, too. It had just popped out as something she felt she owed him.

"But, uh…" Aiden glanced towards the doorway. "You don't have to tell everyone right away. Maybe at least wait until after I go home?"

"Yeah. I'm definitely not going to make a big announcement," she said. "I'll mention it as nonchalantly as possible, make sure it's clear to everyone that it was my decision – as you said – and that no one's heartbroken."

"Good. Thanks." He grabbed her for a friendly hug. Though she was still mildly unsettled by the sensation of having her feet off the ground, it was more comfortable than the hug before they'd cleared the air. Then he motioned for her to lead the way to join the others in the tired debate about how many times someone needed to hear a good tune to know it wouldn't immediately get old.

John and Anna were getting ready to take their little ones home. Eve got to hold the baby for a minute before Anna took her back to get her in her car seat. Aiden stayed for a game with the rest of the family. It went longer than anyone expected. By the time it was over, everyone was ready to call it a night. Matt had only a few seconds to revel in his victory before Aiden went home and the Donnellys went to bed.

Eve had missed the young adult group at St. Jude's. She'd missed Ben. She wondered what the topic for the night had been. She wondered if Ben knew she missed the meeting for family instead of work. He hadn't called her. It was later than they usually talked after the meetings. Was it too late to call him?

The phone lay on her bed with a screen as blank as her mind. What was she supposed to do to fix this? She and Ben were friends, and they were free to be friends. But if there was nothing else between them, then finding out she was engaged wouldn't have changed anything. Simon wouldn't have chastised her if Ben wasn't affected by the news. And Ben would have called her by now.

Eve picked up the phone and called him. Voicemail. "Hey, Ben. Drew got home from school last night so I hung around the family today. I'd love to hear what saint you talked about without me, especially your take on it. I guess it's too late tonight. Call me tomorrow. I'm working early so I'll be home after six."

There was some sort of Advent thing at the church in the morning. Eve's mom left early to make sure her volunteers were in place. She dragged James with her as a backup. Matt and her dad were still upstairs when Eve sat at the breakfast table with Drew. She knew it could be days before the two of them were so conveniently alone again.

"Drew?"

His eyes moved from the back of a cereal box to her face while the spoon continued to his mouth.

She wanted to say it and get it over with, but the quiet words in her head sounded like an announcement. How could she turn it into a casual statement?

"Are you trying to ask me something by telepathy?" Drew said dryly. "Because it's not working."

The bit of humor could keep it light if she said it now. "I broke up with Aiden."

Drew gave a tiny nod of acknowledgment, then put his eyes back on the colorful box and continued eating.

Was he upset? Taking a minute to process it? Eve didn't want to draw out the conversation, but she didn't want to drop it if something was going to fester. "Are you mad?" she asked.

He didn't look at her. He said, "I'm only mad if I'm involved."

141

Eve frowned at his answer. She was his sister, and she'd just broken up with his best friend. That meant he was involved. Yet he sounded as though he intended to be reassuring. "What do you mean?" she asked.

His eyes returned to hers. "You're not going to make drama out of it, right? Like try to get me to talk to him for you or pretend you're fine while constantly asking if he's dating anyone else?"

"Of course not," she said. "I just thought you'd want to know, and you were so excited about me making Aiden officially part of the family. I don't want you to be mad he's not."

"I was excited. It's a nice idea." He shrugged. "But if it's not gonna work, then it's not gonna work."

"Aiden wanted you to know I'm the one who ended it even though he's fine with it, too."

"Everyone's fine?" Drew asked.

She nodded.

"So we can stop talking about it?"

She nodded again.

"Good. Tell me what you think of this stupid math." He turned the cereal box to face her. "These shapes are supposed to represent numbers, but the answer has you use addition when there's no symbols and no symbols means multiplication."

Eve gladly moved on to what should have been a neutral topic, though her brother was clearly more emotional about the stupid math than what they discussed first. He must not have been surprised by it. Matt came down a bit later and said he'd already decided not to eat any of that cereal until the box was redesigned to something that made sense.

When she finished breakfast, Eve saw that Ben had texted in response to her call the previous night. He said he skipped the meeting so she'd have to ask someone else about the topic. It sounded as though he was letting her know he wasn't going to call her later. Didn't he know she'd want to talk even if they couldn't talk about the meeting? Maybe he didn't. And maybe he thought she enjoyed stringing him along. She needed to explain.

She had plenty of time before work. Maybe Ben was available. She tried his number and got voicemail again. "Hey, Ben. I still want to talk even if you don't know which saint or if... uh... I guess you don't have time now though. Call me later, okay?"

Eve took extra time getting ready for work. She pulled those growing bangs into a neat French braid rather than covering them with a headband. She had to wear the red uniform shirt, but it was a good color for her complexion and she added a silver necklace. She hoped that putting together her outside might help her inside be less shaky. It didn't. But maybe it would keep others from noticing.

Eve was at Pans and Plates before it opened to do some prep. When she went to unlock the front door, Jojo was already waiting.

"Come on in," she said. "You hungry?"

Jojo slipped through the door and bowed deeply to greet her.

She dipped her head in return.

He pointed towards the back and nodded vigorously, which she interpreted as him being very hungry. Eve rushed behind the counter to guess what toppings he wanted. It was a fun game as the old guy gave exaggerated reactions to indicate his mood. It turned out to be a simple pepperoni day. She guided a somewhat new employee through getting it ready.

The afternoon stayed busy. Eve was grateful for the activity that kept her from thinking about Ben. That was easiest when she found time to ask Dan if he'd seen how many customers wanted him to draw something special for them.

"People need to stop suggesting things," he said. "There won't be any ideas left, and I'm not going to draw someone else's idea."

"But you will draw something?" His answer no longer sounded like a firm no.

He sighed loudly. "I didn't say that."

"You sound like you're thinking about it," Eve said.

"I didn't say that either." Dan was chopping peppers and not in a position to walk away.

Eve took advantage to continue pressing him. "Come on. You know everyone will love it. Good PR is always good business. And you don't have to use crayons. You can create a mature pencil drawing."

He turned his eyes to her long enough to send a glare.

"It won't take you that long," she said. "No one is expecting a masterpiece, just a fun festive doodle."

"We're not saying festive, remember?" Dan grunted his response.

"Okay. You keep thinking about it. I know a great idea will come to you."

He perked up. "I do have an idea."

"You do?"

"Yeah. You can chop the onions." He put down his knife and moved to get something out of the oven.

Eve was happy he didn't look back to see her laughing. She picked up his knife.

Noah was folding pizza boxes nearby to get ready for the dinner rush. "If you want advice… you should keep poking him, but not too much at once. Letting him get the last word softens him up."

"Now you have advice?" Eve said. "Before you were like, I only have experience *not* talking him into things."

"I have my moments."

There was another area where Eve wanted advice. She really didn't know if Ben was upset with her, and that made it difficult to decide how to approach him. If she was super apologetic when he didn't expect it, would that be admitting guilt? Maybe even make him realize he should be really mad? But if he was upset, and she failed to address that...

Noah was a guy. He might have perspective. "Let me ask you a question about something else," she said. "How upset would you be if you found out Sarah was engaged? I mean, like before you were a couple?"

Noah closed his eyes and paused in his work as his entire body sighed. For a moment, he looked exactly like Dan every time Noah suggested a new idea for the pizza. "I think you're trying to ask me something that doesn't have anything to do with Sarah, and that may not be hypothetical."

"It has to do with Ben."

He resumed folding at a slower pace. He winced as though he was bracing for physical pain. "I know you have a lot of family members who would be just as annoyed to be part of this conversation. Can't you ask one of them?"

"They're not here," she said, "and I'm already asking you." She didn't tell him she'd rather ask him because he probably wouldn't find it flattering, at least not enough to make him more willing.

"Okay. Fine." He let out a sound between a whine and a

sigh. "I know you and Ben have been talking a lot, and it's obvious he likes you. I thought he was just torturing himself. Are you saying he doesn't know you're engaged?"

"Well, he didn't."

"Was that... were you..." He had disappointment in his eyes. "I'm trying to decide if I should be more indignant on behalf of Ben or Aiden. What were you thinking?"

"I wasn't trying to... I don't know how it got complicated." Eve paused to collect her defense. "First, I'm not engaged anymore. Aiden and I have both known for a while that it wasn't working, but... well, I didn't want to do it over the phone. I talked to him yesterday."

Noah gave a tiny nod to acknowledge possible extenuating circumstances.

"I started talking to Ben very innocently. We left one of the meetings at church at the same time. As we were walking out, I asked him what the guys thought was so funny. I remember we could hear you all the way across the hall so all the ladies wondered what was going on over there. Once he started telling me about it, we just kept talking after everyone else went home. I think we must have stood outside the church for at least an hour that night. At some point, I mentioned how I missed a lot of meetings for work, and Ben offered to call me the next time I missed one to tell me what everyone talked about. I really wasn't thinking about anything other than keeping up with the meetings I missed."

"But was *he* thinking something else?" His tone implied there was only one possible answer.

Eve shrugged. She honestly didn't know if Ben had been interested in her from the beginning or if something shifted for him, too. "I don't know," she said. "I did eventually start to

146

suspect he liked me, but… I didn't want to admit it. I felt that telling him I was engaged would be acknowledging there was a reason I should tell him that. I've been just really trying to pretend I didn't notice, that everything was still innocent and not think about it too much." She swiped the back of her hand at a tear that was only partly due to the onion in front of her.

Noah seemed to be counting boxes. He turned back to Eve after a minute. "I didn't hear a question in any of that," he said. "What exactly do you want from me?"

"Ben found out about Aiden from someone else, and I haven't talked to him since. I don't know how much of that is a coincidence. If you were him, how mad would you be?"

"Oh, man." He stared at the ground and fidgeted for a moment before he said, "I don't think I want to try to speak for him."

The situation might be worse than Eve feared. Noah seemed a bit angry just hearing about it. Ben might never speak to her again. She shoved the onions into the bin and put down the knife. She'd chopped enough for now, and it wasn't helping her composure.

"Let me ask you something," Noah said. "Are you just trying to get Ben to help you stop feeling guilty? Or now that Aiden is out of the picture, are you wanting to be with him?"

"I like Ben," she admitted.

"Lead with that," Noah said, "and I'm not giving any more advice." He moved a stack of boxes to block him from her view.

*B*en didn't call the moment Eve got home from work, and he still hadn't called an hour later. She hadn't specified a certain time, which meant she couldn't rule out him being busy and still planning to call later. She also couldn't rule out the possibility that he'd skipped the Friday meeting to avoid her.

The house was quiet. Her brothers had gone to meet Aiden and a few other guys to do some sort of guy thing. Her parents hadn't turned on the TV. They were chatting about some Christmas plans and present ideas. It had seemed like a good time to leave them alone. Eve went into her bedroom, shut the door, and thought about how it was a great time to talk to Ben. If only he would cooperate.

She thought about texting him first to ask if she could call. What if he said no? If she called, and he didn't answer, at least she could say something in a message.

"Hi, Eve."

He answered! She was too surprised to say anything at first. "Uh… uh, hi."

"How was work?"

"Pretty good. Um… I still haven't talked Dan into a Christmas picture, but Noah thinks he's softening."

"Okay. Busy?"

"Yeah. Typical Saturday busy anyway."

The line was silent. Tension radiated in the void. Eve thought her explanation would be easier in person. She really wanted to see him regardless. All she could see when he wasn't in front of her was his sad expression when she'd hesitated to make plans the last time they were together. "I think I want to try shopping again," Eve said. "Can I talk you into coming with me to look at furniture tomorrow afternoon?"

"I… don't think I should."

Eve wanted to start at the beginning, but she had to start somewhere she thought would get Ben to listen. "I know Simon told you I was engaged. But he told you right before I broke up with Aiden. I'm not engaged now, and I really want to see you to tell you why I didn't tell you sooner."

He didn't answer immediately.

"Please," she said. "I can pick you up, and we can talk on the way to the store. I… *please?*"

"Okay. What time?" He sounded more resigned than anything. But at least he sounded willing to listen. He hung up as soon as a time was arranged.

Eve saw Ben at church first, not until she was on her way out. She smiled and waved at him. He returned the smile, but it was clear he was being polite and not happy. Then his eyes found her mom boring down on him and the smile tightened. She reached Ben just ahead of Eve.

"Ben Shannon, you are just the person I was hoping to see today." And she did the glasses thing.

Eve's mom liked to push her glasses down her nose to look over them when she wanted to emphasize eye contact with someone. Her glasses were clear. It made no sense to move them. Yet it appeared to intimidate people all the same. Ben's eyes widened slightly in the trap.

"We only have two people signed up to decorate the church for Christmas. Now we haven't blown a fuse with all the lights yet, but we could always use a qualified electrician on hand just in case."

"Mom, you don't need an electrician to plug in Christmas lights," Eve said.

Her mom continued as though she hadn't heard. "A young, strong electrician would be even more helpful. Someone has to climb the ladder to get the lights and greenery to the top of those pillars." She pointed behind her without breaking her eye contact spell. "Mrs. McGrady is one of our only volunteers so far, and you know she's too old to be climbing ladders. I know you don't want to see that sweet old lady fall and hurt herself, do you?"

Ben shook his head slowly. Wheels were turning behind his eyes as he wondered if not wanting to see Mrs. McGrady fall meant committing himself to saving her.

Eve hooked her arm through her mom's to physically pull her away. "We're not doing the guilt thing, Mom." She called out to Ben. "I'll see you later, and don't worry, my mom is going to find volunteers somewhere else."

His hand came up in a quick wave. There was a hint of gratitude in it. Perhaps this would be a point in Eve's favor when she was trying to convince him not to hate her. Then again, her friendship with Ben might have been what got him on her mom's radar in the first place.

"I wouldn't have to trot out the guilt if you'd have simply smiled at him when I was going with flattery."

"I'm not helping you recruit, as I've said many times," Eve said. "I like it when people are *not* afraid of me."

The comment earned a laugh from Matt, who enjoyed watching his mom recruit from a safe distance so he could make fun of the glasses thing later.

Eve was reminded of her comment about not wanting anyone to be afraid of her when she arrived at Ben's house after lunch. He must have been watching for her because he came outside before she made it halfway to the front door. His expression wasn't fearful, but it was definitely guarded. That wasn't better.

"Hi," she said, trying to sound cheerful.

"How far are we headed?"

"Maybe twenty minutes or so."

He nodded and stopped near her.

The temperature was barely above freezing, but it was the awkwardness that made Eve want to rush back to her car. "Let's go," she said, already moving that way.

The car hadn't been running long enough to warm up. Eve turned the heat high as soon as she was buckled. At first, that was her reason for not saying anything. Having to shout over the vent would not make the conversation more comfortable. Once it was blowing warm air, and she turned it down, the delay had made her more tongue-tied. She worried that the distraction of driving would cause her to fumble her words. But what if there were no right words? What if her explanation only upset him more? Was she about to drag an angry guy into a furniture store? That sounded like the setup for the worst joke ever.

"You said you wanted to talk on the way," Ben said.

Eve felt herself jump. He'd been so quiet she expected him to continue waiting for her to start. "I did," she said. "And I do. I... um... I'm collecting my thoughts." She didn't intend to make him wait the entire drive, especially after he'd prompted her. By the time she got her head around what she wanted to say first, she was turning onto the last street and trying to find the right place amid a strip of colorful signs. Ben still hadn't said anything else as she pulled into a parking spot. She put the car in park but didn't shut it off. If Ben let her, she might talk long enough that they'd both want the heat on.

"As long as we haven't gotten to the door, we're still on the way, right?" She managed a quick smile with her attempt at humor.

Ben simply nodded in agreement.

Eve released her seatbelt and pulled her knee up to turn sideways to face him. "I want to start at the beginning. Can I tell you everything?"

"I don't know what *everything* is so I don't know if there's anything I don't want to hear." He lifted one shoulder in half a shrug. "I guess you can tell me what you want to tell me though."

"Aiden has been a friend to my whole family since before I can remember, especially Drew, they're the same age. Actually, do you remember Drew and Aiden Stevenson from high school? They were only a year behind you."

"Yeah. A little."

"He was always at our house. Aiden doesn't have any siblings so he was happy to claim all of Drew's. Especially when they were in high school, he was around so much I sometimes almost thought of him as an extra brother. I didn't have any... well, romantic thoughts of him. Then he and Drew went away for

152

college. They go to the same school. And I didn't see as much of him for a while. Then I graduated and switched to full time at Pans and Plates. And I started thinking about all the big questions. Do I want to work here forever? Do I want to stay in Andauk? Is there something that would make me regret not going to college? Do I want to have a family? All the things about life, you know?"

Ben nodded that he was still listening, though his eyes narrowed in puzzlement over the new direction.

"I started thinking about Aiden again, wondering if I missed an opportunity. I do want to get married and have kids and I thought about how convenient it would be to fall for a guy I already knew fit in with my family and went to the same church and... I think I got kind of enamored with the idea of that relationship more than him personally.

"The summer before last, he and Drew were home from school and Aiden asked me if I'd ever thought about us, like as a couple. I think he'd been having the same thoughts I had about how easy it could be and maybe being away from me for a while... I don't know, but anyway we started dating. Everyone was *so* excited about it. My brothers were joking almost from the first date about how Aiden would finally be family and not just *like* family. We got caught up in the excitement, and we sort of... This is so embarrassing and juvenile, but it was almost like we got engaged by accident."

Ben's eyebrows went up. "By accident?"

"I know. I was younger, but..." She winced and looked away as she described it. "Near the end of that summer, Drew asked us both if we were ready to make Aiden officially part of the family. He looked at me like, 'Are we?' I said, 'I don't know. Are you proposing?' And he said something like, 'I might be.' So I

153

said, 'I might be saying yes.' I don't think either of us was entirely kidding, but I also don't think we would have treated it like a real proposal if Drew hadn't immediately told my parents and everyone else that we were engaged. Then it felt – at least to me – like we had to be. And being engaged sounded exciting so I didn't think it was bad."

Eve peeked at Ben to gauge his reaction. His expression was mostly unreadable. She didn't see anything in his eyes that suggested she was terrible or unforgivable so she continued her story.

"Aiden went back to school and at first, we called each other almost every day. But we quickly started to run out of things to talk about. There were times I called him just because I knew I hadn't called in a few days or even a week, and by the end of the school year, we'd fallen into a pattern of talking every Wednesday. I didn't realize at the time how obligatory it felt. This is hindsight talking now. He came home the next summer, last summer, and he had a different job with longer hours. I think we only saw each other three, maybe four, times the entire summer. And I wasn't calling him because I didn't have to when he was local. When we got together the last time, it had finally dawned on me – or rather, I finally admitted to myself – that neither of us was trying. Yes, we were both busy, but there were plenty of times we could have seen each other, or at least talked, if we had both wanted to. I should have broken up with him then, but honestly, I just chickened out. And I knew even then that I was more afraid of disappointing my family than I was of hurting Aiden, which I hope was because I could tell he wasn't… Well, he has since admitted he was ready for it to be over, too."

"Why did you wait so long?" Ben asked. "If you knew you didn't want to marry him last summer… I mean, it's December."

"I still don't know if that was the right call," Eve said. "After we went back to the weekly calls with him at school, it seemed kind of dishonest not to say it wasn't going to work out, but… but I just felt even more strongly that he deserved a face-to-face breakup. And I couldn't do that until we were face-to-face."

Ben tilted his head as he listened. He seemed to acknowledge her argument without agreeing with it.

Eve kept talking. "I wasn't pretending to like talking to him or anything because he's a nice guy and I like being friends with him, if we still can. And waiting until the end of the semester didn't seem that long until…" This was going to be the part that included the guy in front of her. Eve's face grew warmer and her voice quieter. "…until you and I started to become friends. I didn't expect… I just thought it'd be nice to have someone fill me in on the meetings I missed. Then I started to look forward to hearing from you more than I should have. I thought you might…" She turned to look at the floor again. "I couldn't say, 'You have to wait until I break up with Aiden before you can ask me out,' because obviously I couldn't say that. It would have been disrespectful to Aiden for anyone else to know before he did. And it wouldn't go very far for having you trust me if you knew what I did to him."

She heard Ben take a deep breath and gladly paused to hear what he might say. Had she convinced him she'd been trying to do the right thing even as she failed? She didn't know what he needed to hear to forgive her.

"You didn't tell me you were engaged," he said, "because you didn't want me to stop calling you?"

"Yes, and I know that wasn't right." She finally looked him in the eye again. It was difficult, but she wanted to show her sincerity. "I didn't know how to say we could only be friends without saying, without at least hinting, that I thought there could be more because... I mean, I could only speak for me, and I wasn't at liberty to do that. I didn't know if you... I *still* don't know if you would even want that." The admission filled her with fear that he might answer – and not give the one she wanted – and she tried not to let him. She abruptly said they should go in the store while she pulled her keys out and grabbed for her purse.

"Eve." Ben's hand closed over hers as it closed over the purse strap and before the other one could open the door to escape. "I do want... more."

"So you can forgive me for not telling... I don't even know. *Should* I have told you?"

"I didn't like being blindsided by it," Ben said. "But I can't honestly say, knowing what I know now, that I wish I knew sooner. Because I would have stopped calling and... Can we... just try to move on from here?"

Eve nodded, though she wasn't entirely satisfied. She still felt unsettled and wanted to ask if he understood she had no lingering feelings for Aiden. She wanted to ask if he felt she'd left anything out. Was there anything that kept him from trusting her now?

He squeezed her hand gently before he let go to exit the car. "Now I need to be honest with you," he said, "and admit I'm not exactly looking forward to this whole shopping thing."

She smiled to herself as she got out to join him crossing the parking lot. Ben didn't want to look at couches, but he wanted to be with her looking at couches. That bit of honesty made the future more promising.

156

****

The store was huge and bright. The other stores Eve tried had partial walls built all over the place. They'd felt somewhat mazelike as she'd wandered from sample room to sample room inspecting possible furniture layouts. In sharp contrast, this store was wide open. The bright lights seemed to highlight the white walls on the far side of the space. Eve took a moment to blink and get her bearings. The furniture was organized into types. Dining tables and chairs were immediately in front of her, and rows of beds were along a near side.

"I think couches are over there." Ben pointed.

They began to walk that direction before Eve located the destination with her eyes. They wound their way through a minefield of coffee tables. Eve was successful, but Ben caught his shin on one. That probably didn't help his enthusiasm for the trip. He followed her quietly and patiently once she reached the couches and began to comment on them.

"That's way too big."

"I don't like that pattern."

"I want one where the pillows are attached to the back because I'm afraid they'll get bunchy if they're loose."

"Whoa! Why is this couch more than twice as expensive as the others? Never mind. I'm moving on."

"Is this broken? No, I don't think… It's just a weirdly asymmetrical couch. No one wants that."

Ben nodded and smiled as they walked. He was listening and even seemed amused by most of what she said, though he didn't reply in words.

Eve wanted a comment on the asymmetrical couch. "Seriously," she said, "what do you think of that?"

"I'm not a fan," he said.

That was sufficient agreement for her to continue. She ruled out the next one on account of it being boring.

Ben laughed at that. "The way you dismiss some of these by what feature jumps out at you... that kind of sounds like you're looking for a boring couch."

"Not this kind of boring," Eve said. "Or this one because it's... Wait a minute. This is the same couch, isn't it?" Her eyes went back and forth to confirm that she was looking at two couches that were the same except for the color. The first was a muted rose while the second was better described as dusty beige. She discovered a third like the others in a dirty sage green. "Okay. What is with these colors?" she said.

"I'm guessing you don't like them." Ben sounded interested in her opinion rather than criticizing her for criticizing the colors. He wasn't calling her picky again.

"All three of these look as though they've been covered with fabric that's been heavily worn and maybe sitting in the sun for a few years. Why would someone want a new couch that already looks old?"

He paused to give her rhetorical question unexpected thought. "I can kind of see the appeal of furniture that looks like it's been around for a while. It could have a psychological effect of feeling familiar as soon as you bring it into your house."

Eve considered that. When she looked at Ben, she could see the appeal. When she looked at the furniture, she could not. "I think you have a point but that these couches are not doing pretend familiar right."

He laughed again. "Yeah. I didn't say I liked this particular shade of not-really-green."

The next piece that caught Eve's eye seemed promising at first, the right size and not an ugly color. But then she ran her hand along the armrest. "Oh. This is so rough. I think I could accidentally hurt myself, like rug burn, just sitting down on this thing."

Ben touched the back of the couch and nodded. "I think someone was going for durability over comfort here. It feels like something you'd put where you felt seating was necessary but you didn't really want people to linger. I don't know, maybe a hotel lobby."

Eve smiled at the idea of a falsely inviting couch. And even more at the fact that Ben was trying to participate rather than standing next to her letting himself be bored. "I think you'd regret taking a nap on this when you woke up with that dense weave pattern imprinted on the side of your face."

"It's like an attack couch," Ben joked. "Maybe you should get it to keep your brothers out."

"That only works if it doesn't keep me out." She moved on to something that made her exclaim was hideous. It had an unusually high back with something almost like a wooden canopy jutting out the top. That was followed by something bland, which she did not observe out loud because Ben might have said the same thing as when she called one boring.

There was a tan couch with blue, green and yellow flowers. At first, Eve thought it was too colorful. After giving it a minute, she appreciated the way the colors blended in a watercolor effect that wasn't as bold as it could have been. She touched the plush

159

fabric and deemed it acceptable for taking a seat. "I need a break," she said.

"Me, too." Ben flopped down next to her. "I'm exhausted from walking all the way over here." He was looking back at the front door that wasn't that far. They'd been walking very slowly.

Eve playfully rolled her eyes at his sarcasm. "I mean a mental break. This feels like a big decision, and it's hard to think about something big too long."

He sat quietly a moment, letting her have her break. Then he said, "By the way, thank you for rescuing me from your mom this morning."

"You're welcome," she said. "I was actually thinking about volunteering myself to help with the decorating. I think it might be fun."

"If your mom tells me you'll be there, she won't need any other arguments."

Eve felt herself melting at the compliment. She tried to keep her wits with humor. "You mean she wouldn't have to suggest you're the only person at the church capable of operating an electrical outlet?"

"It sounds silly and easy to refute when you say it," Ben said. "But when she's looking at you with that intense stare, the only thought in your head is, 'Don't contradict this woman. She *knows* things.'"

"She does know how to convince people to volunteer." As Eve thought about her mom's reputation as the scary volunteer lady, she realized how often she heard respect in the voices of people who said they were afraid of her. "And a lot of times when I hear people talking about how she practically tricked them into doing something, they're also saying they're glad she did it, that they

felt good about giving time and liked being part of something good."

Ben nodded with the sentiment. "I admit I had an ulterior motive when I helped with those Thanksgiving boxes, but I ended up having a blast. Your brothers carried the boxes like they were bumper cars, very controlled bumper cars, and kept colliding with everyone... gently so there was no actual risk of damage. There was a woman there who kept eyeing us like we might lose our heads and ram a wall any second. But even she, in the end, said it was nice to see people enjoying the work."

That ulterior motive threatened to bring red to Eve's face, but they were interrupted by an employee before she thought about it enough.

"Good afternoon, folks," the man said. "Is there anything I can help you with?"

"Not yet," Eve said. "I'm still browsing."

"If you see anything that's *almost* what you want, there are a few options not on display." He fingered a tag on a couch closer to him. "These tags will tell you if there are other colors or sometimes even a reclining option."

"Thank you," Eve said. She'd only been looking at the prices on those tags.

He was older than Eve, though probably not much over thirty. He had clean-cut hair and wore a suit and a thick black wedding band that stood out because it matched his suit, and because it was thick and black. The man pulled a business card out of his coat pocket and handed it to Eve. "If you decide on something or have questions about anything, just text me the product number on the tag, and I'll come and help you out."

Eve said, "Okay," and held onto the card she didn't expect to use.

"Commission," Ben muttered as he walked away.

"Probably," Eve agreed. "It didn't feel like a hard sell, but I kind of wish he hadn't said that thing about the tags."

"Pointing out different colors?"

"Yes. I'm having enough trouble with this decision. I don't think more options is what I need."

Ben smiled with hesitation in his eyes. It seemed he didn't want to agree too strongly that she was being indecisive or appear overly amused by it. "I think your... um... what were you calling it? The dining room that isn't a dining room? I think you've been spending time in there. Does something feel missing?"

"A comfortable place to sit," she said. "Obviously. That's why we're here. I have upgraded from the floor to a hard chair, but I think I can do even better."

"Is it necessarily a couch?" he asked. "Maybe you actually want armchairs, and that's why couches don't seem right. If you think about sitting in that room, what do you picture sitting on?"

Eve wanted to tell him that she didn't know, that she was sure they'd already had a conversation very similar to this one, that they were looking at things she couldn't picture on her own, that she just didn't know. But she tried to think about that room anyway. She tried to picture those yellow walls that Ben helped her paint, and she could almost see them around her. She could imagine being surrounded by those walls as she sat talking to Ben on a couch with flowers that reminded her of watercolor and firm cushions covered with velvety soft material. "What do you think of this one?" she asked.

He pointed under them and raised his eyebrows in a question.

162

It was possible he thought she was looking somewhere else and possible he was stalling to make up his mind.

"Yes, the one we're sitting on," she said.

"It's comfortable."

"And the flower pattern? Do you like it?"

He shrugged and repeated. "It's comfortable."

"Oh, no. You hate it."

"I didn't say that," Ben said.

"You pretty much did. When you dodge a question, it means you have a *bad* answer." She poked his arm as she accused him. "It's like if I asked if something was a nice color on me and you said you'd had a cheeseburger for dinner."

Ben nearly doubled over with laughter, but he composed himself quickly with a deep breath. "That is not the same thing at all. First, just for the record, all colors look great on you. Second, I did not dodge the question with a completely different topic. I was trying to emphasize that whether or not a couch is comfortable is the most important thing. I think the flowers are fine, but I don't feel strongly about it, and your opinion matters a lot more."

"Thank you for giving yours anyway," Eve said. She did not address the rest of what he'd said because she knew it was a terrible example even as it left her mouth.

"Hey, I don't want to crowd you guys if you're still thinking." The salesman was back. "I forgot to mention before though that we have a ten percent off promotion I should be able to apply to just about anything if you're a new customer. I wanted to let you know in case you're on the fence."

Maybe the guy was good at covering up the smarmy, but he didn't come off like someone trying to make a buck no matter what.

He came off like a guy trying to support a family by selling people things they really wanted. That pushed Eve off the fence.

"I want this one," she said.

.

$\mathcal{E}$ ve hadn't known how long to expect it to take to have a couch delivered. But she'd still been surprised it took only two days. It was scheduled for later in the day so she tried not to think about it in the morning. The house emptied early as her younger brothers left for school, her dad for work and Drew began a two-hour drive to visit Mary Catherine and meet her parents.

Eve opened a huge jigsaw puzzle on the kitchen table. Partly because of the turmoil of the pending breakup and denying her interest in Ben, she felt she hadn't taken time to truly relax in quite some time. Perhaps assembling a field of wildflowers on a summer day was exactly what she needed to fill the time before her new purchase arrived. There had been another dusting of snow, but the sunlight streaming through the windows was so bright she could imagine it was as warm outside as it was in the picture.

Eve's mom sat down to help her with the puzzle off and on. A few comments over the weekend had assured Eve that news of her split with Aiden had spread to the rest of her family without her having to endure more conversations about it. No one seemed terribly upset or even surprised. But she remembered what her mom had said about worrying someone would get hurt. She took the opportunity alone with her to let her know that Aiden was fine and agreed they were better as friends.

"And what about Ben?" she asked.

"He knows everything now," Eve said. "I think he's okay with it."

"I meant are you and Ben better as friends?" Her mom kept her glasses in place and gave no intense stare. This was the gentler off-duty version.

Eve chose her words carefully. She and Ben hadn't made anything official, and she didn't want to repeat the mistake of rushing anything. Neither did she want to appear to be hiding a relationship. "So far, Mom. We're friends so far, but I hope… I think we both hope to have a future together."

She didn't press for details. Her expression lacked any trace of curiosity, which suggested she didn't need to ask.

The puzzle was just over halfway completed when Matt and James got home from school. They both hovered around the table adding pieces until they began to argue over whether finding sources for a research paper or writing an original poem was worse homework. Then they went off to dispatch those odious tasks.

The noise of a big truck on the street caught Eve's attention as her brothers' debate left the room. She rushed to a front window to see if it was her couch. The truck had stopped and two guys got out. One went to open the back while the other approached the door. Eve was grinning so big when she let him in that the cold air hurt her teeth. She kept smiling on the inside while she hugged herself and showed him where the new furniture should be placed.

Eve's mom stood with her by the window to watch the guys lower the liftgate. Once it hit the pavement, they made a few circles around the couch. Neither appeared as eager as Eve to get it into the house. One of the guys jumped back into the truck while the other stood by waiting. Eventually, they were carrying the couch towards Eve. It was covered in plastic so she couldn't see it very well. She tried to see through the plastic as it came through the door. It seemed to be the right one.

The delivery guys set it exactly where she wanted it. One began to remove all the shipping protection while the other asked her to sign for it. Then he helped his partner take all the debris back to the truck with them. Eve's mom escorted them to the door. Eve stood marveling at the major improvement to her definitely-not-a-dining-room. It looked better here than it had at the store. There wasn't a lot of yellow in the pattern, but it matched the wall perfectly.

"I like it." Her mom was back and nodding with satisfaction.

James came into the room, shrugged at the couch, then left again. Eve was satisfied with his reaction. She didn't want anyone to hate her choice, but she didn't want any of her brothers to like this couch better than the one in the living room either.

"Can I try it out?"

Eve gestured to her mom to take a seat as she did the same.

"Comfy." She ran a hand over the fabric next to her and smiled. She nodded again. "You made a good choice."

Her mom's approval wasn't necessary, but Eve enjoyed it nonetheless. She thought the couch was more comfortable at home than it had been at the store, too. The two of them sat silently being comfortable for at least a full minute before her mom stood again.

"I'll leave you to bask in the newness while I start dinner."

"Do you want me to help?"

"Not yet. When it gets closer, I might give you a job or two."

Eve pulled her legs up next to her as she leaned against the arm. She might bring that pillow back down now that she had a place for it. She would need a small table next to the couch. Something with a drawer where she could store her bible. She was frequently trying to remember where she left it. There was an outlet there. She could leave her phone charging on her personal table rather than with everyone else's in the kitchen.

The room didn't need much else. It was small enough that it would feel cluttered if she stuffed it with furniture. But a piece of artwork on the opposite wall would be a great touch. A Divine Mercy image maybe? No. She wanted something with more of a story to it. Lots of artists had depicted Jesus calming the stormy sea. Eve was sure she could find a print of one that she liked. The sunny walls as the backdrop for a storm would be an amazing contrast.

She went for her phone and brought the charger, too, even though there wasn't a table for it yet. She wanted to start browsing artwork, but first she needed to check the feed for Pans and Plates.

There had been a huge development on Monday. While Eve was at work and bugging Dan about drawing a picture for a Christmas pizza, he had admitted he was thinking about it. That, of course, did not mean he was going to do it. But she hadn't had any real hope of talking him into it, and now she did. She decided to wait a day before sharing that quote. It would be met with requests for him to keep thinking. Too much pressure could backfire.

She found a ton of new activity before she added anything. Scanning for the source revealed a post from Dan! He very rarely contributed to the online discussion. And this time he'd added only two words: no previews. The cryptic message had churned up speculation. Some people thought he was nixing Eve's plan to post pictures of the kids' drawings before they went out on boxes. Some people thought he was saying he would draw a picture as long as no one posted a copy of it. That got people wondering how anyone would identify Dan's picture if they got it. A few people said he would put his name on it. One commenter said no sane person would be unable to distinguish a grown man's drawing from a child's.

That comment had prompted a firestorm of terrible pictures that asked, "Did I draw this or did my child?" Fortunately, Dan's honor was defended by people who insisted he'd never scribble or do anything half-heartedly. Eve was amused by all the activity and decided she didn't need to add anything at the moment. She'd barely begun to research art when Matt called her name from the kitchen.

"What?" she called back.

"Mom said we won't be able to have dinner until this puzzle is finished and put away," he said. "You started it so you have to help us."

She had completely forgotten about the puzzle. Eve dropped her phone on her new couch and hurried to the kitchen. Both her dad and her younger brothers were standing over the puzzle so she found a place to stand next to Matt. There was only a big patch of blue sky left to complete, which was not shocking.

Drew came home a minute later, happy but tight-lipped about his day. He was also encouraged to work on the puzzle with the threat of a late dinner. Eve somehow found the chaos as relaxing as when she'd been quietly sitting by herself. She laughed as she was jostled by the reaching and shoving. Elbows constantly pushed into her side, usually by accident.

169

James kept saying, "Why am I the only one trying to eat?"

This was met with a chorus of people explaining that he was *not* working faster than anyone else, and claims of how many pieces each had added since the last time he said it.

When they got down to fewer than ten pieces, Eve stepped back to let her more competitive brothers grab those. Soon all five of them had stepped back to admire the finished picture. Then Eve's mom set a stack of plates on the other end of the table.

The moment of calm switched to a frenzy of activity. Eve and Drew worked together to crumble the puzzle and get it back into the box while the others helped set the table and get the food ready to eat.

There was a line of Advent candles on the mantel rather than a wreath. James lit the first one before the family sat at the table. The prayer was a peaceful pause before Matt read his poem to laughs and friendly jabs at his slant rhymes. The most slanty got groans that delighted him. Eve wondered whether his teacher would be impressed or amused that he'd worked ketchup into a poem about a Greek tragedy.

The rest of the meal was pleasant. Eve got a few more compliments on the addition to her room, though her mom was still the most enthusiastic. A game was proposed afterwards. Eve chose to return to her new couch. Ben was going to call her when he was available in the evening, and she didn't want to make everyone pause the game if he called before it finished.

His name flashed on her screen almost as soon as she sat down.

"You have perfect timing," she said as she answered. "I just finished dinner."

"Me, too. Can I come over to talk?"

"Yeah. That'd be great." She smiled. The request was unexpected but very welcome.

"All right. I'll be there in a few minutes."

Eve had spent all day in sweats, but it was a matching set she thought was as cute as it was comfortable. There was no reason to change. She did run upstairs to brush dinner from her teeth and breath. She mentioned to her family that Ben was coming over to see her new couch. They knew he'd been there when she picked it out. There were several snorts and raised eyebrows as the consensus was that it was not the couch he was coming to see.

She didn't mind the teasing as it appeared no one cared about the flimsy excuse. She'd spent so much time worried she'd disappoint everyone by not bringing Aiden into the family only to discover they'd be just as happy to welcome Ben, if it ever came to that. How had she convinced herself her own happiness mattered less to her family?

It probably still qualified as a few minutes, but they were unusually long minutes as Eve paced from yellow wall to yellow wall until she heard footsteps on the porch. She opened the door barely a second after he knocked. She expected him to comment that she must have seen him coming.

Instead, he said, "You don't have to keep it if you don't like it."

"Keep what?" Eve was confused because he wasn't holding anything.

He took a nervous breath and then stepped to the side where he'd evidently left something out of sight. He stepped back holding a small round end table.

Eve wanted to get a better look at it. She motioned him to get inside quickly where she could study it in light and warmth.

Ben set it in the middle of the room where she could walk around it while he explained. "We closed on a new house last week and just today started cleaning it out. It's a place that's been empty for years, and the attic was full of mostly garbage. But I found this under some of the garbage. I cleaned it up really well, scrubbed hard to get all the dust out of the crevices, which damaged the finish in a few places. It was already so worn I figured you'd want to refinish or paint it anyway and… if you want it at all. It must be pretty old because the drawer doesn't have guides and it sticks a little. But it doesn't wobble and seems sturdy despite the skinny legs."

Eve studied the table while he described it. The top was a perfect circle, which her mind naturally compared to the size of a medium pizza. A drawer that was a smaller square fit into it. The drawer was still large enough for her bible and maybe a few pens and odds and ends. It did stick when she pulled it out, more on one side than the other. She was sure it was one of those things that would hardly be noticeable with a practiced technique. There was a shelf below the drawer. If she kept her phone there, she could put something decorative on top.

"What do you think?" Ben asked. "If you start telling me about a cheeseburger, I'll understand."

She laughed at the reference to her example dodge. "I love it!" she said. "Let me see how it fits." She moved it to the end of the couch where she'd already thought to put a table. It was just right.

"We have a few colors of stain on hand if you want to redo the finish. I could even do it for you if it's not an experience you're looking for."

"No, it's great the way it is. The marks add character."

He tipped his head as though trying to decide if she was just being nice.

"Really. Remember how you were saying people make new things look old on purpose like they're already familiar…" She pointed at the table. "That's how you do it right."

"Except that it's not a new thing trying to look old," he said. "It's just old."

"Even better. Every mark is part of a beautiful history."

"Which part of the beautiful history involves being stuffed in an attic and forgotten under piles of garbage?"

Eve frowned playfully at him. "Are you *trying* to talk me out of liking it?"

"I'm just giving you all the reasons it's okay with me if you don't like it."

Even though Eve was enjoying the banter, she wanted to give it a serious turn. She was still sensitive that his trust might have been damaged finding out about Aiden from someone other than her. "I'm thinking that I shouldn't have to tell you I love it more than once before you believe me."

"That's an interesting point." Ben's eyes widened as he appeared flooded with thought. "Do you remember a few months ago at St. Jude's… I don't remember how the discussion started, but we… we talked quite a bit about fear being the opposite of joy, how not trusting God causes fear and… fear robs us of joy. I'm seeing this as a tiny trivial example. I was afraid you wouldn't like it and expected you to not like it and… Anyway, you're right. I'm going to choose to believe that you actually want that table."

Eve nodded at the logic. She remembered bits of that discussion and tried to recall more. "Well… now that you believe me, I can say thank you for it." She gave him a quick hug.

As she pulled away, his hand gently touched the side of her face to keep her from backing too far. "I feel like I want to thank *you* now, but I'd only be, uh… thanking you for being you." His eyes scrunched as though that was ridiculous.

Eve thought it was sweet. And the way he was looking at her was more than sweet. It enveloped her with a feeling that the moment was part of a new beautiful history. It also made it hard to talk. "You can, um, thank me… if you want to."

He accepted the invitation with a soft kiss to her lips. His hand moved from her face through her hair and made her spine shiver with delight.

Ben took a step backwards as soon as he was done. His eyes glanced towards the kitchen where several of her family members burst out laughing about something she could not – at that moment – care less about. She kind of wanted to thank him for the kiss to start a loop where he "thanked" her again. Instead, she asked if he'd seen all the buzz about Dan's comment. He had not. Eve directed him to take a seat on the couch as she pulled out her phone to relate some of the highlights next to him.

"I like this guy," she said. "He's like, 'Dan is a professional. He would only use *sharp* crayons.' And I think this is unintentionally hilarious. This person practically wrote a dissertation on how the 'charm' of kids' drawings is lost when they are digitized because she thinks Dan doesn't want me to share them online, and I don't even think that's what he meant."

Ben had thrown his coat aside when they sat down to review the posts. He was closer than he'd been at the store to see over her shoulder. Eve again found herself thinking the couch was better now that it belonged to her. They began to guess which pictures were drawn by adults.

174

"I think this one might actually be the work of a six-year-old," Ben said. "The way Santa is so much bigger than the other people seems like a child's perspective."

"*Or...* it's an adult like you thinking a child would make Santa bigger."

Ben winced at her point. "Oh, it might be. And I might have fallen for it."

"Honestly, I'd vote child, too," Eve said, "even if it could have been a tricky adult."

"That one's got to be an adult." Ben pointed at the next picture. "I know it's just scribbles, but it's too... controlled."

Eve nodded. She didn't think a toddler could make the lines so even. "This one is interesting." She paused to consider a holly wreath. "Most of these people seem to be submitting intentionally bad drawings, but this is pretty good. Is she showing off a talented 5-year-old or... maybe just couldn't bring herself to draw something worse?"

"You're right. Most of the pictures are going with the assumption that adults draw better than children," Ben observed. "But that's only true to a point. Eventually, talent and time spent practicing become more important than age."

A notification popped up about a text from Noah.

"Go ahead and check it," Ben said, turning his head to offer privacy.

"Oh my gosh!" Eve enjoyed the text and shared it with Ben. "Dan did draw a Christmas picture, and it's wonderful. Noah says his dad can't believe anyone misinterpreted his comment that so obviously meant no one could see his picture ahead of time so I have to hang onto this to post after the original is delivered. It's great."

Ben laughed as she zoomed in on different parts of the picture to appreciate it. Dan had drawn Santa in front of a line of stockings. There were pizza boxes sticking out of his bag and several of the stockings. In his hand was a lump of coal he was about to drop in a stocking labeled Noah. There was a caption that said, "Top of the naughty list this year."

"Hey, guys, do you want to join us for *7 Wonders*?" Matt was standing in the doorway holding the game box. "We'd have all seven then."

Eve looked at Ben and saw a hopeful question mirrored in his eyes. "Yes." She jumped up and Ben followed her. After the game – that Eve won by one point – Ben said he needed to get home. She walked him to the door.

"Because of all the time I spent cleaning that old table, Nate thinks I need to haul everything else out of the attic by myself tomorrow. It might be a long day."

"Maybe you'll find some other hidden treasure," Eve said.

He shook his head doubtfully. "I'm just going to be happy if I don't find rats or tetanus."

Eve shuddered. "I have to work Friday night this week so if I don't hear from you before then, I'll be expecting a call about everything I miss at church."

"I'm pretty sure you're going to hear from me before then." He reached for her hand and gave it a squeeze before he moved to open the door.

"Good night." Eve waved before she closed the door behind him. Then she moved to a window to wave again. He didn't look back until he was in his car. Then they shared another wave before he drove away.

Eve stepped into her yellow room and gave a contented sigh. The round table in the corner drew her eye, and she moved to brush her fingertips across its surface. She felt tiny scratches and imperfections. It was as though she could feel the time Ben had spent cleaning it. The fact that it was a gift of time made it more valuable than anything new. She would find the right thing to sit on top of it and a perfectly stormy picture for the wall. There were a few details she hadn't figured out, but she had confidence that she would find joy in this room. Ben had already played a part with his paint and table. She smiled as she wondered if God would use him to bring even more joy to her life.

~~ The End ~~

Find out about upcoming books, read excerpts with notes from the author, watch various covers take shape, and much more at www.amandahammbooks.com.

www.ingramcontent.com/pod-product-compliance
Lightning Source LLC
Chambersburg PA
CBHW020124180626
46810CB00004B/1401